First published as Gone: The Felicity Lawrence Series in 2018 by Claire Taylor using CompletelyNovel

Copyright © Claire Taylor 2018

Claire Taylor has asserted her right under the Copyright, Designs and Patents Act 1988 to b identified as the author of this work.

This book is a work of fiction and, except in the case of historical fact, any resemblance to actual persons, living or dead, is purely coincidental.

Every effort has been made to obtain the necessary permissions with reference to copyright material, both illustrative and quoted. We apologise for any omissions in this respect and will be pleased to make the appropriate acknowledgements in any future edition.

ISBN

9781787232372

Gone

The Felicity Lawrence

Series

Book Two

Claire Taylor

More Books Written By Claire Taylor

Murder At First Sight

Soon To Be Released:

Winters Kill

Praise For Murder At First Sight: The Felicity Lawrence Series Book One

"... a good solid bet if you are looking for a thriller with some interesting characters, perfect for reading on a train or plane journey. Am looking forward to next in the series. (hint! Hint! Claire).

"It was short and punchy which made me sad when I finished it so quickly... I would recommend it as a good teenage read although equally enjoyable for adults."

"... a quick, easy to follow, novella like crime mystery that is a nice light read"

Prologue

Taking a deep breath, he pulls at the balaclava, feeling around for skin, making sure he is completely hidden.

When he is happy that nobody will recognise him, or even see him through the thick blackness, he pushes slowly through the door of the shed. As the cold air hits his face, he closes his eyes for a moment with relief. He has been crouched in there for hours, knowing that nobody would discover him.

Opening his eyes, he looks up and rests his gaze upon her bedroom window. He remembers every step to that room, which stair to avoid so that the creaking doesn't wake anybody. He has been there before.

As he approaches the back door, he quietly slips off his shoes, and pushes the key into the lock, turning it slowly, heart racing faster with every click that it makes.

He hoists the small rucksack onto his shoulder, feeling the roll of tape shift. He didn't think that he would need it but... just in case.

Finally, her door. Slightly ajar, so that her mother could hear if she woke up. The soft blue night light casting a moonlight glow upon the cream carpet of the landing. The door swings open at the touch of his fingertips, and he just catches it, heart skipping a beat.

Somehow he is across the room in seconds, and he kneels beside her for a moment bathed in moonlight.

Chapter One

Felicity perched heavily at the end of her mothers' bed, gazing around at the room, eyes resting upon photographs of the two of them at the beach, the park, beside the tree at Christmas.

Barely a month had passed since Felicity's mum had been sent to the hospital, unconscious and fighting for her life. Every day she had been to visit her, hugging her and talking to her, although she had no idea whether she could hear her. They told her that she could, the nurses and doctors. She half suspected that it was just a way of making her feel better though.

They all spoke about her in secret, or so they thought. She could tell, though and sometimes she heard them whispering. It was as though she had committed the murders, and not her awful teacher. The one that everybody had loved, and so doubted as a murderer of teenage girls.

Felicity had made a statement with Ella standing defiantly beside her, leaning against a crutch, her leg still a little painful. Noah Bennett in the background with Ruth and a row of other police officers who had supposedly played a part in the investigation. When it had played out on the local news, the camera seemed to linger on his face watching her as she spoke, admiration, pride and something… else passing over him. They didn't really talk about the something else.

She sighed again and stood abruptly, smoothing out the creases that she had made in the quilt. In just three weeks,

Felicity would be moving away to university. Should be. Goodness knows what she would do if her mum was still in the coma by then.

Of course, the police had been pushing the whole idea of working with them. They had training programmes in the village, they said. She knew that they meant well, that they thought that this was her calling. Mostly, anyway. Most of them seemed to think that she could call the dreams at will. That she was one of 'those people' who could touch a bracelet, or a photograph of the victim, and summon visions, solving the case in seconds.

Slowly, she wandered across the hall and into her own room. Everything seemed way too normal. Her clothes were still slung over the back of the chair. Her suede brogues were still just under the bed, the toes peeking out at her. She had barely been in this room since… everything.

Kicking her plimsolls off, she threw herself onto the bed and stared up at the ceiling until her vision blurred. She started at the sound of her phone vibrating.

"Hi, El'" Felicity clicked her best friend onto loud speaker, hardly having the energy to lift the phone to her ear.

"Hey!' Felicity could hear the smile in Ella's voice, as she silently thanked the stars that she had such a positive best friend, 'how's your mum?"

"She's ok, no better, but no worse' She rolled onto her side, 'I've been reading her favourite books to her every day. And playing her favourite music. They say that she can hear everything" She noticed that she sounded more hopeful than convinced.

"She's strong Fliss, she'll be just fine. Do you want me to come over? Or you could come out? We can go to the Shake Shack, have some dinner. I've barely seen you".

It was true, Felicity thought, considering her options. She hadn't seen Ella for days, Ella was preparing for University, spending lots of time with her family before she left. And Felicity was pretty much living at the hospital.

"Ok,' she relented, not wanting to be on her own tonight, 'we'll get dinner."

She held the phone away from her ear, laughing as Ella squealed her delight, "Yay, do you want me to pick you up?"

"No that's ok, I'll walk, I could use the fresh air".

Almost feeling as though she had a new lease of life, Felicity tried to gain some control over her hair, serving only to pin the wild curls around her face behind her ears, and swept on a little mascara. She pushed away the guilt that she was feeling; she was allowed to enjoy herself every once in a while.

*

She stood, staring at it, the wind biting at her ears and cheeks. It suddenly felt unseasonably cold for August, as though she were being chilled to the bone.

The barn loomed above her, a weather-beaten 'for sale' sign beside the fencing, leaning precariously on its' post. In the distance, she could still see a strip of police tape flapping in the wind.

Felicity hugged her arms across her chest. She hated being here, and seein g it, and somehow, no matter where she was going, she would always end up walking past, as if her feet took her there without her mind being privy to the decision.

She could see, as if she were having a strange, out of body experience, all of them running from the barn toward the Moors; Mr. Geoffreys at the front, Ella's limp body slung over his shoulder. Herself chasing desperately after them, legs pumping like never before, and Noah close behind.

Noah.

If she let herself think it she would say that she loved him. But she couldn't think it, and so she wouldn't. She hadn't spoken to him in weeks. It was almost as though this huge, life changing thing that they had experienced together had actually driven them further apart. She didn't know how to thank him for saving her life. And neither of them knew how to deal with their feelings.

She missed him. Taking a deep breath and blowing it out in one quick blast, she shook everything from her mind, and walked briskly away from her past.

*

Chapter Two

"You made it!" Ella jumped up, her blonde hair bouncing about her shoulders. She looked fantastic, her legs brown in a defiantly short skirt. She refused to let what she had been through stop her from taking over the world, or so she chanted to Felicity every moment that she could. She would wear her hideous scar with pride.

Felicity nodded, throwing her arms around her oldest and best friend. She felt as though she were more relaxed just by being around her, "I missed you El!"

"I missed you too!' Ella slid into the booth, pushing a menu towards her, 'I'm sorry I've been such a rubbish friend. What's going on with you? How is Noah?" She waggled her eyebrows comically, and Felicity tried to ignore the thud of her heart hitting the ground.

"You tell me' She sighed, forcing a half smile for her friends' benefit, 'we haven't spoken since… a few days after it happened. I miss him."

"Oh Fliss. Men are idiots, they -" Ella stopped suddenly, momentarily (and rarely) speechless.

"El?' Felicity turned her head to follow Ella's eyeline, and immediately noticed the source of distraction, 'who is that?"

Ella shook her head, watching him as he pulled on an apron and picked up a pen and pad, "I don't know but I think it's time to order, don't you?"

Before Felicity could stop her, Ella had thrown her hand into the air, forcing eye contact with him.

"Hi' He smiled softly, before turning to Felicity and gazing into her eyes for a moment, 'what can I get for you?"

Felicity watched him curiously while Ella ordered for them both; he had dark brown hair, and eyes that were such a deep brown they were almost black. He seemed to have a permanent smile on his face, as if he were never angry or sad. She wondered whether she should just start looking at other guys in that way again; she was at least allowed to admire them, enjoy their company, maybe even flirt a little bit.

She tried to imagine herself flirting with the waiter, smiling coquettishly, fluttering her eyelashes. She rolled her eyes – she wouldn't know how to flirt if it would save her life.

"So, his name is Callum' Ella leaned in toward her as he moved away, her eyes bright, 'he just moved here, he's the same age as us. Don is his uncle which explains how he has a job here so soon after moving in"

Felicity looked at her friend incredulously, amazed that she could have found out so much information in such a short space of time. "I don't know how you do it" She mused, shaking her head.

"It's a gift' Ella grinned 'we are also showing him around the village tomorrow"

Felicity snorted. The village consisted of a small field (or a patch of grass to most people) in the centre, with paths that surrounded it. There was one pub, a newsagent, a village hall and two 'tourist' shops. A small library was perched on the edge of the carpark. Shake Shack was the most exciting and modern place to arrive in the village. Ella rolled her eyes.

*

Noah Bennett had had a relatively quiet summer. He had mostly been dealing with local robberies (of which there were few) and, one exciting night, a noise complaint. He had almost been tempted to slip into the party that had been the source of said noise just for something more interesting than the ham and pickle sandwich that he had eaten for lunch.

Not that he wanted a murder popping up around every corner, but he hadn't become a police officer so that he could complete mundane paperwork every day. He supposed that what he really wanted was a distraction; something to occupy his mind so that he didn't think about Felicity anymore.

He wasn't sure what had happened, where they had gone wrong. It was as if, in the hours after the awful event, they became closer than ever, Noah supporting Felicity through the trauma of her mother and her best friend, and Felicity checking in on him constantly, icing his bruises and thanking him with tears in her eyes for saving their lives.

And then, almost within the same number of hours, it had all changed. They both seemed to become... embarrassed?

Vulnerable? That was probably it, he mused, inwardly shaking his head. Neither of them wanted to appear as if they needed anybody else. So, they each backed off, and the more that the other person backed off, the more they gave each other space until it seemed as though they would be starting again if they spoke now.

"Officer Bennett?' Noah started as Ruth peered at him around the door, before beckoning her in, 'we have a call out for a kidnapping."

He watched Ruth as she led the way, striding importantly in front of him. Maybe he should have let her seduce him. Maybe they weren't such a bad idea. They got along, she was beautiful. And they both understood the job, how much time it could take up. Maybe, it wasn't too late, he mused.

She still seemed to like him; she flirted with him if they went out for a drink, and once recently it had seemed as though she had been about to kiss him. She was a little older than him, only by a few years, but she had just enough experience that he could learn to be a better person. But with Felicity he didn't have to learn, he was already better. Well that was too bad, he told himself crossly.

He shook his head as Ruth stopped, glancing back at him expectantly. He had his work to focus on.

*

Felicity watched Ella drive away, waving enthusiastically before turning towards her unwelcoming, empty home. Her smile dropped and her heart rate quickened a little. The street light outside her house was flickering, casting strange shadows in the darkness.

Taking a deep breath, she moved quickly towards the door, almost running to close the gap. She fumbled for a moment before pushing her key into the hole.

She froze as something moved behind her, a cracking sound ringing out into the silence. Slowly, she turned, squinting to see into the pitch black around her. A whistle started up in her ears as she held her breath, trying to hear every little sound.

After a moment, she decided that she must have imagined it. Blowing out a shaky puff of air, she turned the key in the door, and pushed her way in, pulling the door to a close behind her.

And as she moved through the house, switching lights on and off as she went, he moved from his hiding place in the bushes, took one last look at her through the upstairs window, and stepped silently away.

*

Felicity stood in the doorway of her mothers' bedroom, her arms wrapped around her body, her pyjamas and her dressing gown on. She had lay in her own bed for a couple of hours now, struggling to sleep, as she did most nights now-a-days. She needed her mum home.

She moved into the room, sighing as her bones creaked along with the bed as she clambered on. If she really focused, she thought, burying her face into the pillow, she could almost smell her. Closing her eyes, she imagined that her mum was there with her, arms wrapped around her and telling her that everything would be ok.

*

Chapter Three

As they pulled up outside the house, Noah could see a pale, gaunt face in the orange light of the streetlamp. The mother, he thought.

Unbuckling and climbing out, he made haste to meet her, shaking her hand gently "Evening Mrs. Baker. I'm Officer Bennett, and this is Officer Christy. Shall we head inside?"

She nodded, barely acknowledging that they were there. As they followed her up the long garden path, Noah peered at his surroundings. Nice house, the path lined with carefully cut bushes. But the front lawn was a little overgrown, the tips of the blades dry and brown.

Stepping in through the large front door, they blinked rapidly in the sudden brightness of the house, eyes adjusting to the change of light. There was a faint murmuring from somewhere in the house, and they followed it, Mrs. Baker leading the way.

"Oh good, you're here,' a plump, elderly woman beckoned them into the kitchen before hurriedly placing mugs of tea on placemats on the breakfast bar, 'I've made about twenty cups of tea waiting for you"

"I'm sorry Mam, we came as quickly as we could,' Ruth reassured her calmly, 'I know that it's a stressful situation but -"

"Oh no dear, you got here in double quick time, you really did. I'm just so nervous I needed to do something with my hands,' she indicated their mugs, pushing one gently towards Mrs. Baker, 'drink up everyone."

"Thank you" Noah murmured, obediently sipping, trying to ignore the layer of skin that he had just taken with it.

There was silence for a moment as they all seemed to adjust to each-others company.

"So, Mrs. Baker -"

"Ms,' She looked up sharply, her eyes flashing with anger, 'it's Ms."

"I'm sorry. Ms. Baker' Ruth corrected softly, her professional veil never dropping, 'when was the last time you saw your daughter?"

"Bella" A tear slipped slowly down her nose and off the tip.

"When was the last time you saw Bella?"

Mrs. Baker looked at them desperately, "When I put her to bed. No, it was a little bit later, when I went to bed. I checked in on her. She was sleeping. She was asleep."

Noah pulled out his notebook, scribbling quickly. "Were there any signs of forced entry? Broken locks? Was her bedroom window open?"

"No, nothing. Everything was the same. I don't know how this could have happened, I'm so careful, I - " Her head fell into her hands, her voice breaking and then dropping away completely.

"It's ok sweetheart' the elderly woman wrapped her arms around her, forehead creasing with concern, 'we'll find her. They'll find her. Won't you?"

She looked at them desperately, "You'll find my granddaughter, won't you?"

Noah and Ruth glanced at each other, hearts sinking.

"We'll try' Noah ran a hand through his hair, and tried to be reassuring, smiling softly, 'we really will try."

There was a brittle silence for a moment; nobody wanted to break it for fear that everything might shatter.

"Mrs. Baker,' Ruth ventured, finally, 'how old is your daughter?"

"Um, she's six, six years old.' A breathless sob escaped her lips, and she pressed the back of her hand to them, 'she'll be so scared, please help her!"

"Is there anybody that might want to hurt you? Anybody holding a grudge?"

She shook her head helplessly, looking almost as though she wished there was.

Noah cleared his throat, "Mrs. Baker, do you mind if we take a look in her room?"

She hesitated for a moment before nodding reluctantly. Noah offered a kind smile in return before following her up the stairs.

The door was wide open, pushed right back against the wall as though flung in desperation.

As they entered through a doorway of pink fairy lights, they were met with the typical bedroom of a six - year old girl. The bed had a pale pink canopy over the top of it, with a floral bedspread which was still creased where her body had been. The carpet was also pink. Teddy bears and dolls adorned the room on the bed, on shelves and the window ledge. One particularly worn bear lay on the floor, curled up on its' side as if he had slipped from sleepy little fingers.

Noah felt sadness and fear tug at his stomach as he took everything in, picturing the happy little girl from the photographs on the shelves downstairs. What if they couldn't find her in time? He shook his head, pulling on a pair of gloves; he wouldn't let self – doubt get the better of him.

*

Chapter Four

"Well that was tough' Ruth sighed, her eyes flicking between Noah and the road, 'was that your first kidnapping case?"

Noah nodded, watching the road disappear beneath them in front of him. This was both the part of police work that he hated, and the reason that he had become a police officer in the first place; didn't they all do it to help people?

"Do you want me to drop you at home? I can pick you up in the morning."

Noah shook his head, "That's ok, I'm going to head in and finish a few things up"

Ruth flashed him a look of concern, "Don't overdo it Noah, you won't be treated like a hero if you collapse with exhaustion one day"

He rolled his eyes, "I won't mother,' he grinned, 'I promise I won't be more than twenty minutes, and I'll leave."

A smile played about his partners lips as she pulled into the car park, swinging into a space gracefully. "Fine, I'll ring you in twenty, and you had better be leaving!"

He laughed, shaking his head as he made his way across the car park, lifting a hand to her as he disappeared through the front door of the station.

It was eerily quiet, just the low hum of a vacuum cleaner in one of the distant rooms. Most of the lights were switched off, with just a few desk lamps casting a dim glow around the main office.

Clearing his throat, a nervous habit that he was trying to kick, Noah made his way to his desk at the back of the office, switching on his own desk lamp. He sat for a moment, the leather of his chair creaking under the weight of him. Ruth was right, he was spending too many late nights there. Some might say he was trying to distract himself.

And distract myself I will, he told himself, shoving some papers into a file. He logged his notes from the case onto the system before glancing at his watch and realising, with a smile, that he only had five minutes left on the clock.

Easing himself out of the chair with a sigh, he made his way along the back corridors of the station, the darkness swallowing him up; there was minimal lighting down here, with a few flickering bulbs hanging from the ceiling.

Suddenly, in the silent black, every footstep sounded louder, bouncing off the walls. He slowed as he approached the filing room. It almost sounded as though there were two sets of footsteps.

He ducked inside, yanking at the light switch so that it sprung up from his hand, the light flicking on suddenly. He made his way deeper into the cupboard, finding the shelf that he needed and quickly putting the files away.

A shadow moved by the door, looming across the floor for a moment before melting away into the dark corners of the room. Noah froze, his entire body tingling. There was silence for a moment, before slow footsteps began to ring out into the air.

The shadow flashed across the ground again closer this time. Noah's heart was racing now, as he went into alert mode, patting his pockets and realising that he didn't have his gun.

His breathing was becoming heavy and laboured, and he tried to calm down, convincing himself that he can handle it, this is what he was trained for.

The shadow was one shelf away, making its' way around the corner – a scream erupted from the shadow as his phone began to ring shrilly and at top volume. There was a loud crash, and Noah peered cautiously around the shelves of files to see the cleaner; a slight, pale young woman who right at this moment was looking terrified, hurriedly gathering up an armful of cleaning products.

"I'm so sorry, are you ok?" He handed her the last few items, trying to ignore the heat in his cheeks.

With one final apology, Noah slipped out of the room, practically running along the corridor. His phone began to ring again, echoing through the long space, and he answered, grateful to hear Ruth's laughing voice at the other end, telling him that he was five minutes late, and he owed her breakfast.

As he drove away, scolding himself for working so hard that he was going mad, he didn't look into his rear-view mirror; and if he had, he would have seen the dark, broad figure all in black slip out of the door, closing it carefully behind them, and followed moments later by an unsuspecting cleaner.

*

She could see a blurred face; a man's face she thought. And he was crying, sobbing in fact, the tears streaming down his cheeks.

She was standing, but looking up at him. She felt a strange combination of feelings – she loved him, but she was also terrified of him right at that moment.

She searched frantically for a mirror, a glass table, or a reflective surface of some kind.

There was a lot of noise; shouting voices. Suddenly the man grabbed her, pulling her so that he had his arm across her chest, holding her tightly in place. His free hand was wielding something shiny. She tried to follow it to see her reflection, but she could only catch a distorted glimpse of her freckly cheek, a small scar near her nose.

And Felicity sat, drawing in a long, rasping breath, sweat dripping from her hair, and soaking through her clothes. Dread filled her body as she realised. It has happened again. Another one.

*

Chapter Five

Noah rubbed his eyes, staring at the file but barely seeing it, he had been looking at it for so long. Ruth was pacing the room in front of him, chewing her thumb.

"When will we get results of the evidence back?" Ruth stopped, glancing up at him desperately.

Noah shook his head and shrugged, "Soon, I hope. It's in there now. Is there anybody that we haven't considered, or spoken to?"

Ruth took the file, flicking through it quickly before suddenly pausing on a page about halfway through, "The dad. We haven't spoken to the dad!"

Noah dropped his face into his hands; of course, they should have spoken to the dad. He glanced at the clock. Eight a.m.

"O.k,' he stood, pulling his jacket on and shoving the file into his bag, 'let's go"

Ruth followed his lead, striding along the corridor, heels clacking against the linoleum.

As the large, station doors creaked open, and the fresh morning air hit their tired faces, they stopped simultaneously at the top of the steps, appreciating being outside for a moment.

They had been there all night; for reasons unknown, neither of them could step away from this case, even for a few hours. It had been so long since they had slept, that Noah was starting to feel delirious. He was fairly sure that he had just seen Felicity on the opposite side of the car park.

Rubbing his eyes, he climbed into the drivers' seat, checking the address that they had for the father.

"Noah!" He blinked, trying to work out where the voice was coming from.

A hard rap on the window sent both of them flying out of their seats, and he turned, swallowing his shock at the sight of Felicity Lawrence's beautiful, and worried face staring at him, indicating that he should roll down his window.

"Hi"

"Hi" She smiled shyly, and they watched each other for a few moments, hearts pulsing in their throats.

Ruth cleared her throat awkwardly staring at her knees to hide her discomfort.

"So,' Noah leaned toward Felicity trying to talk over the uneasiness, 'what's going on?"

"It's happened again" Her forehead was creased with worry, her voice rushed.

"What?!" His breathing seemed to lighten, and fear pooled in his stomach. This was a small village, the murders, and attempted murder before the summer break, had dented it severely, affecting the tourism as well as losing them a few locals. Another murder might ruin it altogether.

"I've had another dream,' she looked at him, a pained expression upon her face, 'I think that I was young, a child. Or just very small. I couldn't really see my reflection. Just a scar by my upper lip." She shook her head.

Noah sat up, a strange feeling flooding his chest; like when you were about to do something exhilarating, and you didn't know whether you were going to love it or hate it. "Did you see who the killer was?"

She shook her head, "Not really. It was definitely a man. But the face was blurry, and from my angle it was hard to tell how tall he was or anything like that."

"Listen,' he turned deliberately away from Ruth, knowing that she would be annoyed that he was about to share information with Felicity, 'we have a little girl missing, six, blonde hair, blue eyes, scar above the lip. We have zero leads right now, so if you get anything else. Anything at all. Let me know"

She nodded, stepping away from the car as Ruth started the engine. Swallowing the lump in her throat, Felicity turned and made to walk away.

"Felicity' Ruth's clear voice rang out at her, and she turned, smiling brightly, 'don't take it upon yourself to investigate this. Please? You almost killed yourself last time, please just leave it to us. Unless you want to rethink joining us that is?"

Ruth raised an eyebrow, grinning, "Oh, and don't share the details with anybody else. Not even Ella!"

Felicity nodded, and Noah could see her watching them as they drove away.

*

Chapter Six

Ella bounced on her toes, her hair springing at her shoulders. Felicity smiled fondly, but it didn't quite reach her eyes, she knew. They were showing Callum, the new boy as Ella fondly referred to him, around the village, but since her dream Felicity's heart just wasn't in it.

"Penny for your thoughts?" A voice murmured softly beside her ear, and she started before turning awarding Callum a tired half-smile.

"Sorry, is it that obvious?' she shook her head apologetically, 'I just had… a weird dream last night that's all. I'm just a bit tired and I can't seem to shake it you know?"

He nodded, pushing his hands into his pockets. "Thanks for showing me around today' he glanced down at her before taking a look around at the village, 'I mean, I think I can see it all from here but…"

He grinned and she couldn't help but return it with one of her own, "Hey, it might be small but it's perfectly formed!"

Callum laughed, and dimples appeared in his cheeks, "When my parents told me that I had to move here for the summer, I was devastated,' he shook his head, amused, 'I haven't even been here since I was about eight, so it wasn't as though I even had any clear memory of it. I just felt that it would be the middle of nowhere, and I would be hanging out with my uncle, or with old people all day long."

"And what do you think now?" She looked up at him expectantly.

His dark brown eyes, pierced into hers for a moment, and she wasn't quite sure how she felt about it, "I think it's looking up."

"Hey!' Ella bounded over to them, her slim legs brown in her denim shorts, 'what are you two talking about? Hurry up there's lots to see Callum!"

She pushed herself between them, hooking her arms through theirs and pulling them across the field and toward the little, thatch - roofed pub with it's textured, white walls and the lavender climbing up to the traditional patterned windows at the top.

"A little pub lunch to kick off the day?" She grinned at them, her hair swishing behind her as she looked at them alternately.

As they made their way inside, people were already sitting at tables outside, sipping beers and ciders, enjoying the sunshine that was beating down on their shoulders. They could hear children screeching with laughter in the garden at the back, and the happy chatter of people enjoying a break, the last of the summer.

This is how she remembered the village, Felicity thought to herself, happiness mingling with the sad undertone of a good thing that has been spoiled. Before murders, and coma's, and complicated relationships (or non-relationships) with good-looking policemen.

At the back of the gardens was a stream which bleeds into the river which then runs to the lake. Ella led them to her favourite table right at the edge of it, and they sat, Ella leaning back in her seat for a moment, eyes closed blissfully against the sun.

Felicity could feel beads of sweat spring up at the back of her neck, and she scooped her unruly curls into a pile on top of her head, fastening it with an elastic band. Callum had taken their orders and headed inside to buy, his treat.

"So…' Ella smiled lasciviously, and Felicity rolled her eyes in a premeditated response, 'you and Callum seem to be getting along well."

"Don't start' she tried to glare at her, attempting to cover up her amusement, 'I barely know him, and even when I do know him, it will just be as a friend!"

They glanced across the garden as he appeared from the stable door exit, a tray of drinks in his hand, and the sunlight hitting him just right.

"If you say so" Ella murmured, admiration and laughter dripping from her words.

*

Noah peered out of the window at the dingy, ramshackle house. It was big, that was for sure, but he couldn't imagine any sane person choosing to live here. It reeked of dilapidation and danger. He wasn't sure that he really wanted to get out of the car, but Ruth was already making her way up the path with its' broken paving stones.

"Nice place" He murmured sarcastically into Ruth's ear as he caught up with her.

She raised a brow at him, pressing the doorbell as she did so, before realising that it was broken and rapping smartly on the wooden door.

For a few moments there was silence, and then cautious footsteps began to approach followed by a shadowed outline growing bigger the closer it got. The door opened a crack, and a tired, pale blue eye filled the space.

"Mr. Baker?" Ruth stared back at him passively.

"Can I help?" He asked exasperatedly; he sounded weary, as though he thought that he definitely couldn't help.

"Can we come in?"

He watched them for a moment through the crack, before letting out a barely audible sigh and pulling the door wide open. He turned and shuffled into the house, gesturing at them to follow.

Though bare, the interior was surprisingly clean and neat. On the wall in the hallway was one solitary picture; a framed photograph of Mr. Baker, Lynette Baker and their daughter Bella, arms wrapped around each other, eyes crinkled with laughter. Noah wondered briefly what had happened to that happy family.

They were taken into the living room, which held a small, grey sofa, a tiny television and little round table in between. It was small, but tidy, and Noah began to feel a little more at ease.

"Mr. Baker…" Noah began, sitting forward on the sofa.

"Please, call me Matthew" He interrupted, smiling softly.

"Matthew, has Mrs. Baker been in touch with you recently?"

He frowned, leaning closer to them, "No, why, is she ok?"

"She's fine' Ruth reassured him, pausing for a moment as if she didn't want to tell him what she was going to tell him, 'Matthew, it's about Bella. I'm afraid that your daughter is missing."

Noah watched him carefully, trying to gauge his reaction. What he saw, almost as though in slow motion, was the breaking of a man's heart. Matthews face crumpled, his breathing quickened, and he blinked into the empty space in front of him for a moment as though he were trying to gather himself together.

"Well how long for? What are you doing about it?"

"I can assure you that we are doing everything that we can' Noah smiled in what he hoped was a comforting manner, 'we are waiting for results back from the lab for her bedroom, and we have had police officers questioning the neighbours, asking whether they have seen anything strange."

Matthew nodded, dashing away a tear that had made its' way over his lower eyelid.

"Matthew' Ruth looked at him through half – closed eyes, as though she were concentrating, 'when was the last time you saw Bella?"

He dropped his head into his hands before drawing his fingers down his face, and peering up at them miserably, "Months ago. Twelve months ago."

*

Chapter Seven

It took Felicity a moment to work out that her phone ringing had been her sudden wake-up call. She rubbed her eyes, her other hand feeling around blindly until it found the phone.

"Hello?" She murmured, trying to work out what time it was.

"Are we speaking to Miss. Lawrence?"

Felicity sat up, waking up quickly. The voice at the other end of the phone sounded stern and important.

"Yes, speaking"

"Miss. Lawrence, I'm calling from the University of Plymouth. We have met with a bit of a road block, and we need you to come in for a chat. When are you free to come in?" He sounded weary.

"Is something wrong?" Felicity could feel her heart rising in her throat. The prospect of going to university in September was just about the only thing getting her through at the moment.

The man from the university sighed, "Miss. Lawrence, I'm afraid that I don't know the details, I just make the calls."

"Ok' she climbed out of bed and pulled apart the curtains. The sun was beaming, mocking her, 'ok, I can come in this afternoon?"

There was a pause, and Felicity listened hard, trying to decide whether they had hung up or not.

"Two o'clock?"

She nodded, then realised that he couldn't see her, "Two o'clock is fine."

"We'll see you in two hours".

She stared at the phone as he clicked off. Two hours. She sighed. It was going to be one of those days.

*

Felicity tried to hold her bag against her body as she ran at full speed down the station steps. She could hear the train pulling up to the platform, and she tried to move her feet even faster.

People seemed to be pushing in front of her, turning into a soup that she struggled to push herself through.

"Come on!" She muttered, earning herself a few glances as she began to force her way between people. She could see the carriage doors opening now, and people beginning to climb on.

Springing off the bottom step, she began to pound the platform, eyes fixed upon the doors that she knew would close at any moment.

A message began to ring out, telling them that the doors were about to close, and she pushed herself a little bit harder, her breath ragged and tearing in her chest.

She breathed a sigh of relief as her toe touched into the train, and she grabbed the bar to pull herself in. Catching her reflection in the glass beside her, she held back a groan; her face was a strange dark red, her curls had created a frizzy cloud around her head, and a bead of sweat was trickling down her hairline. And she only had half an hour to get there.

Luckily, the train journey was relatively short, and it wasn't too long before she was carried out on a sea of passengers and onto the streets of Plymouth. Where it was raining. A lot.

Tucking herself under the shelter of the entrance, she glanced down at the strappy summer dress that she had pulled on this morning whilst looking out at the blazing sun.

She thought for a moment, before taking a deep breath, and sprinting into the downpour, bag held over her head.

Rain sprayed up from the pavement as her feet smacked against the concrete, and she could already feel the back of her dress soaking through.

By the time she broke through the doors of the university, her hair was limp and running rivers down her body. Her dress was dripping a steady rhythm onto the wooden floor, and her plimsolls were squeaking with every step.

The entrance hall was silent, save for the echoing droplets, and the light tapping of the receptionist. Shivering, Felicity approached the desk, peering at the man whose eyes were fixed upon the computer screen.

Suddenly, the eyes flicked up to her face, staying there for a moment, mouth a small 'o' before he gathered himself together. "Miss. Lawrence?"

She nodded, trying to summon a smile.

"Please take a seat, you will be called in in a moment' he indicated towards some low, cushioned seats lined up against the wall, 'can I… can I get you a towel?"

Felicity felt her cheeks redden as she nodded, "That would be great, thank you."

He brought the towel to her, a smile playing about his lips. She was glad that he found it so funny.

As she dabbed herself dry, she gazed around at the university that would become her home in a few short weeks. A fizz of excitement bubbled in her stomach.

"Miss. Lawrence' the receptionist stood before her, smiling and indicating that she should follow, 'this way please."

*

The man on the other side of the large wooden desk in the centre of the sizeable office was middle aged, with a stern face, and a completely serious expression. As soon as she entered the room, making her way to the wooden chair opposite him, she knew that this conversation most definitely wasn't going to be good.

"Miss. Lawrence' he peered at her over his glasses, 'thank you for coming."

She smoothed the skirt of her dress, trying to ignore the fact that it was still wet, and nodded, "It was no trouble."

"Miss. Lawrence, I'll cut to the chase here,' he leaned toward her, resting his chin upon the spire of his fingertips, 'your exam grades were not as good as we had hoped."

Her heart sank, and her mouth filled with saliva. She was going to lose her place at university. She began to panic, opening her mouth to speak. He held up a hand to stop her.

"I understand that you have been through a hard time, particularly around the time of your exams, which is why we have decided to give you a chance that we wouldn't usually give."

She shuffled forward on her seat, her dress sticking to the chair, "Of course, what do I need to do?"

"We have an exam for you to take' he sat back in his chair, looking mildly disappointed, 'it really is a shame Miss. Lawrence. The exam is an hour, and it will start the moment you put pen to paper."

He pushed a booklet of paper and a pen across the desk towards her, smiling.

"An exam?" She felt fear rising in her throat, like bile. Was this really necessary? She was sure that it wasn't usual.

With a shaking hand, Felicity lifted the pen, and slowly placed the tip against the first page.

*

Chapter Eight

Felicity stood with her back to the large doors, listening to them swinging to a close, and the footsteps of the receptionist walking away, before letting out the breath that she had been holding.

She peered up at the sky, with mild irritation and an air of relief. The sun was shining now, beating down on her and springing beads of sweat upon the back of her neck.

As she walked away from the university, she felt as though her chance to leave everything behind and start again was slipping away from her along with the building. She sighed. She would be getting the results of the exam back by the end of the week, but she didn't hold high hopes. She hadn't been able to concentrate, her brain flicking between her mum, and the dream and the possibility that everything was falling apart.

She could feel her dress drying against her skin, and tried to relax and enjoy the warmth. Digging into her bag, she pulled out her phone, scrolling through missed calls. One from Ella, followed by a texted photograph of her on the beach, one from Noah and one from a phone number that she didn't recognise.

She frowned at the screen. Why would Noah be calling? She had told him everything that she knew about her dream. Her finger hovered over the call back symbol, her heart racing.

She jumped as a new call from the unknown number flashed onto her screen, and she held her breath to calm herself down.

"Hello?"

"What are you doing right now?" Callum's voice, amused and strangely loud echoed through to her.

She glanced around at the people bustling around her as she approached the train station, "About to get on a train home from Plymouth."

"Plymouth?' she could hear him moving and wondered briefly what he was doing, 'we're hanging out tonight".

She laughed despite herself; he sounded so definite, so sure, "What if I don't want to?"

"Of-course you want to. You can come to my uncles, he's out tonight. I'll cook dinner, and we'll watch movies."

She felt a grin tug at the corners of her mouth, "You can cook?"

"I can cook' there was a pause, and she pressed the phone closer to her ear, 'at the very least I can order a pizza!"

She chuckled again, "O.K fine, what time?"

"Let's meet at the café at seven? We can walk to my Uncles' house, it's a nice walk"

Hanging up, she made her way into the station and down to the platform; she was feeling much more relaxed than she had on the journey to Plymouth, and she let herself daydream about Callum.

It wasn't that she really liked him that way, not really, not yet at least, but something about him made her feel… happy. Warm inside. God knew that she could use an extra friend at the moment. But no more than a friend, she scolded herself, climbing into an empty carriage and taking a seat. She had learned her lesson with Noah; you fall too quickly, you struggle to get back up again.

She closed her eyes for a moment, erasing that last thought. She wasn't going to let anything ruin her night, after the day that she had had, she deserved to have a bit of fun.

*

Glancing at her watch, Felicity pressed her back against the cold brick wall of the café. The sun was still bright in a vivid blue sky, and she could hear sea gulls squawking, searching for left overs, or kind-hearted diners willing to donate a portion of their meal.

The village was still bustling, fishermen rolling up their sleeves and gulping down pints of beer in the pub garden, milling with the old men who frequented every evening for 'just one' and the students enjoying their last few weeks of freedom before the confines of study and exams once again.

She pushed her hair out of her face, turning it up towards the warmth. She had swapped the wrinkled summer dress for a plain white t-shirt and a mid-length, light-silk, emerald green skirt. She stared at the white plimsolls on her feet, the toes scuffed.

"You came!" Callum's voice lifted with delight as he rounded the corner, having closed up Shake Shack.

Felicity smiled, watching him approach, so that she had to look up at him in the end, his form silhouetted in the sunlight. He wore a dark pair of jeans with a grey t-shirt. He carried a small rucksack, and a basket. "What's that?" She pointed at it curiously.

"Well' he grinned, clearly pleased with himself, and leading her towards the field 'I thought, why order pizza and eat it cooped up inside when the sun shines so brightly? So…"

He stopped just below a large tree, the sunlight dappling through the branches, just the right amount of shade and sun, and opened the basket. He pulled out a soft blanket, throwing it upon the ground with a flourish.

"A picnic!" She exclaimed, curling herself upon the blanket happily.

"And…' he pulled out a laptop, and a stack of DVD's looking at her triumphantly, 'which do you want to watch?"

Felicity laughed before falling upon the films and rifling through them, eventually picking one out that was suitably girly. Callum groaned with exaggeration, pushing it into the laptop.

"Ok, we've got pizza made by my own two hands just moments ago, chunky chips, cut, buttered and salted by myself, and salad if that's your thing."

Felicity smiled, thinking that though she didn't know him very well, and hadn't known him for very long, she was lucky that right at this moment she had him.

For a while they ate in silence, watching the movie, but every now and again they would glance at each other, catching the other persons eye, and smile shyly, edging closer by such a small amount at a time that they almost didn't notice they were doing it.

"So,' he whispered, leaning in so that his breath tickled Felicity's ear, 'why were you in Plymouth?"

She groaned, wanting to forget the whole experience, "University entrance exam. My grades weren't quite what we expected.' She glanced at him, trying to ignore the fact that they were so close their eyelashes could touch, 'it went terribly, I don't want to talk about it."

"Are you ok?"

Felicity nodded, her eyes falling to his mouth. She tore them away, knowing that she shouldn't get involved with anybody, especially somebody that she wasn't even sure that she liked that way, "This is the perfect distraction"

They were silent for a moment, the air suddenly crackling between them. Maybe it was enough, Felicity thought, that they had fun, enjoyed each-others company. They weren't getting married, and besides, he was only here for the summer.

It was growing dark now, the stars twinkling above them, and the lights of the beautiful pub, which was strung with delicate fairy lights, shining behind them, bathing them in a soft glow. The village had quietened down, so that, save for the nineteen-year-old girl who worked at the pub a few nights a week clearing up glasses, Felicity and Callum were the only ones around.

The silence was suddenly palpable, the heat from their bodies seeming to rise in the air cooling around them. Felicity swallowed hard, and she thought that she saw Callum's lower lip tremble.

Carefully, he closed the gap, lips pressing against hers softly. For a moment she did nothing, frozen, and then she sank into it, relaxing against him as his fingers found her hair.

He pulled back, looking a little surprised, eyes searching her face as if making sure she was ok. She nodded, then thought about how strange that was. She could feel her cheeks burning, unsure about what to do next.

Callum smiled fondly, took her hand in his, "Shall I walk you home my lady?"

She grinned relieved; nothing needed to change if she didn't want it to.

*

"This is it' Felicity peered up at her home, the empty house that she would spend the night alone in, and suddenly she wished that the night wasn't over, 'thank you, for the best night I've had in a while"

Callum smiled, nodding his head at her, "My pleasure' he moved toward her so that she could feel him breathing, and gently touched his lips to hers, pulling away quickly, looking at her with curious amusement, 'I've never met a girl quite like you Felicity Lawrence."

Felicity grinned, making her way up the path, turning as she reached the front door, and raising her hand in a wave, "I'll see you later Callum Mires.".

Stepping into the house and closing the door behind her, she paused for a moment, relishing the evening that she had just had, enjoying the residuals of happiness, and normality. She wanted to hold onto those forever.

*

Chapter Nine

Noah stood in the back garden of Lynette and Bella Baker, staring up at Bella's ' bedroom window. He turned in a circle, slowly, taking in everything around him.

The houses in the street are all detached, with a gap of roughly three feet between them. The gardens backed onto gardens of the houses in the street behind, sharing a fence at the end.

Frowning, he jogged over to the fence, pulling himself up so that he had a clear view over the top.

"Ruth' he called, heart jumping a beat with excitement. He turned to look at her as she made her way through the back door, 'Ruth, the neighbour has a clear view of Bella's bedroom window."

She nodded, her loose blonde hair moving in a glossy wave, "We'll speak to Lynette about it first, see whether she has any cause for concern. Then we'll talk to the neighbour."

"It's something though, isn't it?" Noah followed her as she moved quickly across the grass, the tips of her heels sinking into the earth.

"It's a very loose one. But we will investigate it. We just need to work out how to approach it, that's all"

Noah bit down his frustration as they entered the house. Lynette was perched on the edge of the sofa, her face red with recently shed tears, eyes dried out from the salt of the drops already spilt. Her hands clutched a pile of photographs, Bella's face smiling out from them, distorted where she was holding them so tightly.

"Lynette' Noah spoke gently, worried that he might scare her she was so within herself, 'can we talk to you about the neighbour opposite? The one with the garden backing onto yours?"

She looked up at them as if only just noticing that they were there, before nodding, "Tom Carol"

Noah and Ruth sat opposite her, taking out notepads and pens, "Tom Carol? Do you know Tom well, Lynette?"

She shrugged, then frowned, "He worked with Matthew for a while. After they were made redundant, they planned to go into business together. He came over a few times back then but suddenly they stopped talking."

"Do you know why?" Ruth asked.

Lynette shook her head, staring at her knees, "I heard them arguing one day' she admitted, 'Tom stormed out, he was really angry about it."

She looked up at them suddenly, face bewildered, "Do you think that it was Tom? He treated Bella so nicely everytime he met her. He doesn't seem like the type…" She trailed off, perhaps realising that nobody could be trusted anymore, it could be anyone.

Noah stood, smiling softly at her, "We'll just go and talk to Mr. Carol, rule him out. Better to be safe than sorry."

They left Lynette on the same sofa that she had been sitting on since they arrived, with the photographs adorned with her contact details in a desperate bid to find her child.

The summer breeze was refreshing; being in the Baker household was stifling, the grief pressing itself to their faces like thick, suffocating pillows. They would never admit it, not even to each other, though they both knew that it was felt. It seemed cruel to feel that way, when Lynette Baker must feel so much worse.

*

Tom Carol had greeted them with charm, and kindness, and now they were sinking into the soft sofa, steaming mugs of tea in their hands. It was almost as though he had been expecting them.

"It's just so sad,' Tom paused to sip his tea, before looking at them with eyes that held confidence and sympathy, a strange combination, 'she was a sweet little girl"

"Was?" Ruth questioned, those silvery-grey eyes hard.

Tom barely moved, just the twitch of an eyebrow betraying his irritation, "My apologies, is."

Noah wandered over to the wall to wall sliding glass doors leading out to the back garden. From here, he could see a lot of Bella's bedroom, although not quite the bed. "Do you mind if I take a look upstairs Mr. Carol?"

"Tom please' he nodded towards the stairs, not showing any sign of moving from his position on the sofa, 'feel free."

"Could you just show me which room upstairs looks out over the back garden?"

Tom nodded again, eyes narrowing a little, leading them up the stairs and into a large office at the back of the top floor.

Noah and Ruth made their way to the window, and Noah's heart skipped another beat. This room had a perfect view into Bella's bedroom. From here you could also see into the Bakers' kitchen; Nora, Lynette's mother was washing up, staring blankly out of the kitchen window.

"Tom, you seem to have a brilliant view of the Baker house from here."

Tom moved so that he stood beside Noah in the window, matching the direction of his gaze. "So I have,' he shook his head regretfully, 'but I didn't see anything that night I'm afraid."

"Did you ever see anything worth looking at through that window Tom?"

Disgust and anger flashed across Tom Carol's face, and for a moment Noah thought that he was going to hit him, "No' his voice was cold, all trace of friendly welcoming gone 'I'm not that kind of person. Maybe you should be conducting your search for the poor girl properly instead of harassing innocent men."

Ruth smiled cooly, crossing her arms, "You were in business with Matthew Baker weren't you?"

"For a short while"

"And what changed?"

"We just disagreed, it happens sometimes, most business fall at the first hurdle."

"Mrs. Baker described an argument that she heard between the two of you' Ruth watched him carefully, 'said that you were very angry. Angry enough to try to hurt him?"

"Are you suggesting that I kidnapped Matthew's daughter just because we had an argument?"

"Well, maybe the punishment matches the crime?"

"Oh, for goodness sakes,' Tom slammed his mug down onto the desk, tea spraying out onto the wood, 'I put up the money for the business venture, and Matthew wasted every penny of it."

"Gambling?" Noah murmured, more to himself than anyone else, but Tom responded anyway.

"Drink' Tom spat, 'that, and poor business decisions. He wasn't made to run a business of his own. But he was desperate to make money to support Lynette and Bella since the redundancies, and I'd been talking about starting my own business, and he begged to be a part of it."

"How much did you put into the business?"

"That's irrelevant, I don't discuss money" Tom flashed them a look of irritation.

"Would you say it was a Bella – worth amount?" Ruth looked at Tom directly.

Tom shook his head, "Get out of my house" he pushed past them, making his way downstairs and ripping open the front door.

Stepping over the threshold, Noah turned back to him, smiling cheerfully, "We'll be back Mr. Carol."

"What do you think?" He asked in a low hum, turning to Ruth.

"I'm not sure. Something seemed… fake. We'll let him stew for a little while. If he doesn't approach us by tomorrow we'll come back."

Noah glanced back at the house as they rounded the corner. Tom, a small dot, an ant on his doorstep, seemed to raise a mocking hand towards him.

*

Chapter Ten

"You didn't text me back yesterday!" Ella cried the moment Felicity opened the front door, stepping into the house as if it were her own.

"Sorry, sorry. Callum called before I could reply. He wanted to have dinner." She blushed furiously and turned away quickly, pressing her cool hand to her cheek.

"And did you?!" Ella threw an arm over her shoulder, watching her expectantly.

Felicity nodded, making her way through to the kitchen. "We had a picnic and watched Dirty Dancing on the field" She smiled, flicking on the kettle – it was only nine a.m, and coffee was most definitely needed.

Ella grinned, squeezing her friends arm. "It's about time, you need to get over Noah."

"Listen, Noah and I were barely a thing. We were a drop in the ocean. I'm fine."

Ella rolled her eyes "Ok, miss independent, I'm just saying, that instead of moping here in your pyjamas' she raised an eyebrow at the flannel shorts and t-shirt that Felicity was wearing, 'you should be having fun with a boy your own age!"

"Ok mother' Felicity laughed, pouring two coffees, 'I might see him again. We may have shared a little kiss."

Ella cheered, throwing her arms around Felicity until they collapsed into a giggling heap.

For the second time this week, Felicity began to feel lucky. And happy.

*

Lynette picked through the field with its' flattened strands of corn, making her way towards the woods at the back. She had come alone, but she knew that she would soon have company. He had called her this morning, and in her moment of weakness, in her current fragile state, she just needed somebody. Somebody else who was living it.

And there he was, in the distance, moving towards her, jogging a little. He didn't look great, she noticed as he became close enough to see, but he looked better than the last time she had seen him.

"Hi" His voice was soft and careful, as if unsure of where he stood.

"Hi" Her voice cracked and they began to move, closer to the trees, heads down.

"How are you?" He asked shakily.

"Probably the same as you" She laughed. It had been a few days since she had really laughed, and it was rasping and dry in her dusty throat.

Silence again, as the soft corn made way to sticks and mud crunching beneath their feet.

"Do you think she's here?" He tried again, staring around them in horror.

"Maybe, I don't know' Lynette was weary. If her daughter were here, then it would mean that the unthinkable had happened. But even now, after just three days, she was exhausted. She just wanted to know. To know where she was, what had happened. 'Matt, what if we have to do this forever? Not know, look for her every day in the faces of children, and then teenagers and even adults after that, and wonder whether it's her? Or whether she's gone?"

Matthew stopped, taking her shoulders and turning her to face him, "That won't happen. And if it does we'll deal with it."

"Every time a body turns up, and they don't know who it is, we'll wonder whether it's her. We'll have to look at it, try to identify them."

"We'll deal with it Lynn. We have to.' He held out his hand cautiously, 'we'll do it together?"

Hesitantly, she took his hand. Staring at it for a moment, she squeezed it, and then they moved, making their way further into the darkening woods.

*

Chapter Eleven

Felicity stretched her arms up over her head and pushed herself further down into the pillows. The quilt was piled by her feet at end of the bed, and the sunlight was streaming in through the gap in the curtains, covering her legs, bare in a pair of blue cotton pyjama shorts, in a delicious warmth.

The day before had been perfect, just what she needed to forget about the case that she had dreamt about. A part of her wanted to jump straight into it, start investigating and solve it before anything bad happened. But she had been told to stay out of it. The last time she had got involved Noah had ended up hurt, and her mother ended up in a coma.

She sighed; she wasn't going to think about this now. She had been in such a good mood since spending the previous day with Ella, eating and watching movies and just having a girls' day. She wasn't going to let something that was beyond her control ruin it.

She pushed herself out of bed, pulling her curls into a messy bun on top of her head, and pulling the curtains wide open, peering out at the blue skies and the sun beaming over the top of the houses opposite.

She frowned; out of the corner of her eye, a figure moved. The frown swiftly became a smile as Callum came completely into view, grinning up at her and waving enthusiastically.

Pulling a thin yellow sweatshirt over the top of her vest, she made her way down the stairs two at a time wrenching open the front door and revealing Callum, hands in the pockets of his knee-length khaki shorts, skin tanned against his white t-shirt. The deep brown hair was dishevelled in a way that looked good on him, and his eyes were dancing with amusement, so dark that she couldn't see the pupils.

"Good Morning" She said brightly, standing back so that he could come in.

"Morning" He glanced down at her, a smile playing about his lips, and Felicity was suddenly uncomfortably aware of how close he was to her.

"How are you?" Callum's voice was a whisper, low and rasping, his breath warm on her cheek.

"Fine" She breathed. They seem to have moved even closer to each other so that their clothes were touching. She could see each individual eyelash, and the little black speck in part of his iris.

Slowly, he moved his lips to hers, smiling against them. She relaxed into him for a moment before they pulled away from each other.

"Are we going to make a habit out of this?" She teased, leading him into the kitchen.

"I hope so!" Callum laughed, leaning against the breakfast bar. She raised her eyebrows in response, boiling the kettle for coffee's.

"To what do I owe this pleasure?" She asked, perching on a stool opposite, their hands resting casually beside each other across the worktop.

"What are you doing today?" He watched her hopefully as she poured coffee. She really didn't have anything planned for the day ahead. Maybe brooding over the disaster of a university exam, or the dream, or the failed non – relationship with Noah.

"Nothing!" She cried, unable to keep her smile from stretching across her face. This was what she needed, she thought gazing into Callum's sparkling dark eyes. Some fun, something relaxed, just taking each day as it comes.

Callum laughed again, "Ok, well get dressed, we're going out!"

Felicity planted his steaming mug in front of him before making her way as quickly as she could to her bedroom, yanking open her wardrobe doors. After just a few seconds of deliberation, and one last look out of the window to confirm the weather conditions, she settled on a pair of denim shorts, and a pale grey, V-necked t-shirt.

Pulling on some grey converse, she let down her hair, slicked on some mascara, and sprinted down the stairs, leaping the last few two at a time. "Ready"

Callum peered down the corridor, smiling at the sight of her, before climbing slowly off of his stall, and moving towards her. Her stomach began to wriggle with butterflies, as he grew closer, the muscles of his stomach moving beneath his shirt.

He stopped just in front of her, gazing down at her with a sudden passion that she hadn't quite seen yet, and though she wasn't sure where it had come from, she certainly didn't dislike it. Slowly, he put his arms around her waist so that his fingertips were resting on her lower back, and leaned down until his mouth met hers, moving against it slowly but purposefully, as though he meant it.

The kiss deepened, and Felicity suddenly didn't know whether she felt nauseous or excited, but she threw her arms around his neck, telling herself to enjoy it as much as she knew she really did. A smart rapping on the door, drew them apart, and they looked at each other for a moment, breathing heavily.

"Are you going to get that" Callum grinned, running a hand through his hair.

Felicity chuckled, moving her hair from the back of her neck trying to cool down, and pulled open the door, trying, and failing to ignore Callum moving close behind her, hands on her shoulders.

"Felicity, I -" Noah stood on the other side, his words faltering at the sight of Callum behind her, smiling, oblivious to the history between Felicity and this man on her doorstep.

"Hi Noah" Instinctively, she pulled away from Callum a little, not turning to find out whether he had noticed or not.

Noah cleared his throat, arranging his features into a professional expression, "I just wanted to see whether you had any more information?"

"No, I'm sorry. Do you have anything?"

Noah shook his head sadly, "Not really, we've spoken to a couple of people, but really, we don't have anything."

Felicity took a step toward him, reaching out a hand to pat his arm, stopping herself at the last moment. Noah looked at the hand for a moment, before giving an imperceptible shake of the head and plastering on a smile which was so obviously false to Felicity.

"Anyway,' he began to back away down the path, 'I'll leave you to it."

Felicity watched him walk away, her heart sinking. She hadn't thought that he was interested in her anymore, but it had been so awkward, and for a moment he had seemed so… sad. Why did this have to happen just as she was getting over him?

*

Chapter Twelve

Noah leaned back against the bench in the middle of the field, in the centre of the village, and rubbed his face with his hands. Rationally, he was aware that he hadn't exactly built up a good case for himself with Felicity lately, he had pretty much avoided her. But the irrational side of his brain was angry at her for moving on so quickly.

But then they hadn't even been anything had they? So why, then, did it feel as though his heart had just shattered, burning his chest like acid?

Should he call her, he wondered? Ask her to spend time with him. He shook his head. Of course not, he didn't want to make an idiot of himself; she clearly wasn't interested anymore, and he wasn't about to force himself upon her so that she had to openly reject him.

Who was that boy anyway? He shook his head again. He was just torturing himself. He sat up suddenly, pulling out his phone and scrolling through the contact list. If Felicity could have fun with somebody else, then so could he.

*

Hours later, as the day moved into the evening, Noah watched from his seat beside the fire as Ruth entered the pub, looking around for him. She looked lovely. Her blonde hair fell down her back in a cascade of carefully crafted curls. She was wearing a pair of fitted black jeans and a burgundy, silk sleeveless blouse. She wore a pair of black heels, and as she spotted him, she flashed him a smile, her lips painted a dark red.

As she made her way towards him, her hips swayed in time to the clacking of her footsteps, and Noah, who had already had a few drinks, found himself momentarily hypnotised before leaping to his feet and hugging her warmly.

"Oh!' She exclaimed in surprise, and then squeezed him back gently, sitting beside him on the old leather sofa. 'this is nice."

Noah nodded, sliding a glass of vodka and lemonade across the small table in front of them so that it stopped just in front of her.

Taking a sip, she closed her eyes and smiled happily. "Perfect!"

"Good,' Noah watched her for a moment through determined, if slightly blurred, eyes, 'Ruth, I wanted to talk to you."

She placed her drink carefully on the table, peering at him, suddenly concerned "Okay" She spoke slowly, and raised a hand, indicating that he should go ahead and start.

"We've known each other a while' now that he had started, he felt nervous, but he persevered, looking her in the eye, 'and I'm thinking, that we should give us a go."

There was silence for a moment, several different emotions flashing across Ruth's face, "Us?"

"Yes, you and I' He shuffled closer, 'we get along, I find you attractive, and I like spending time with you. I think that this could be… something."

"Noah' she turned her body to face him, frowning, 'what about Felicity?"

He blew out a noisy puff of air, and waved a dismissive hand in front of her face, "We haven't spoken properly for weeks, I don't want her anymore, and she doesn't want me."

Ruth put her head to the side, sighing, "Noah, that isn't true. I know that you haven't spoken for a while, but there is something between you, you can't just let that go."

"She has!" Noah sat back, defeated, and let his face crumple a little.

"What do you mean?"

"I went to see her today, and there was somebody else with her. He looked like he owned her, you know?" He looked up at her, his eyes glistening, and blinked rapidly.

"Did you ask her about him?' Ruth queried. Noah shook his head and she sighed again, 'you need to talk to her Noah. Be a grown up." She was teasing, but there was a serious undertone to her voice.

Noah knew that she was right. He loved Ruth, but just as a friend. He knew that he was just trying to get over Felicity. They both looked up, a little spooked, as Ruth's phone began to trill.

"Ruth speaking?" Noah watched her, her face becoming serious, listening intently.

"What's going on?" He asked as she hung up.

"Tom Carol, he says that he has evidence for us, to prove that he is innocent."

*

Tom was wringing his hands as he invited them in, clearly nervous.

"Ok,' Ruth took the lead as they stepped into the house, 'what do you have for us?"

Tom held out a leaflet; it was pale pink, with black lace print around the bottom and a phone number. Nothing else.

"What is this?" Noah demanded, taking it from him curiously.

"This is where I really was that night' he looked down, clearly uncomfortable, 'take it away, call the number."

"Mr Carol' Ruth took a step toward him, a frown creasing her forehead, 'would you care to explain - "

"No!' Tom held up a firm hand to stop her, turning away from them, 'please just take it, and don't share this information with anybody else."

They stood for a moment, until the silence became too uncomfortable and Ruth and Noah let themselves out.

"Well' Noah murmured, plugging in his seatbelt, 'that was a bit strange."

Ruth shrugged, nodding at the card, "We'd better give that number a call."

*

They had booked an appointment straight away with a voice on the phone who sounded very pleasant, if a little bit young, and made their way there as soon as they had hung up the phone.

The young receptionist had introduced the business as a relaxation bar, but Noah and Ruth both had their doubts regarding the legal merit of the place, and so had decided to drive there in Ruth's inconspicuous Fiat rather than the police car.

The entrance was an inconspicuous black door. They had travelled about an hour out of their village, to a small, and admittedly slightly run-down part of the county. The small sign above the door had a thick layer of black dust covering half of the name, but they could see that they were at the right place, and parked in the one allocated space outside.

"You should go in alone" Ruth turned to him, a small smile playing about her lips.

"What, why?!" Noah groaned, knowing that she was right, but not really wanting to go in at all.

"First of all, it will be weird for us to go in together. This is obviously not the kind of spa that you go to for a relaxing session in the hot tub. And I'm not sure that too many women frequent that door there either."

"That's a little sexist of you" Noah huffed, climbing out anyway, ignoring Ruth's laughter.

A shrill tinkling rang out as he pushed open the door, making him jump, and a woman appeared, smiling softly.

"Welcome' her voice was smooth and sweet, and Noah instantly recognised it as the voice on the phone, 'Noah, is it? Would you prefer anybody in particular? We have no customers at the moment, so everyone is available."

"That's right' He smiled, trying to relax into the role, 'Tom Carol recommended this place to me, so could I have whoever he usually has?"

He watched as she moved over to her computer, tapping the keys and squinting at the screen. She was fairly young, though not as young as he had suspected. Probably early twenties. Her long black hair was pulled back into a ponytail and she had long pink nails which clacked as she typed.

"Ok,' she smiled at him, heading towards a door in the back corner and indicating that he should follow, 'you're all booked in with Maria, Mr. Carols' regular."

He led her along a brightly lit corridor with three doors along each side and one at the end. They stopped outside of the third on the right, and he could hear soft music emanating from inside the room. The receptionist, whose name he hadn't got around to asking for, knocked gently before opening the door, ushering him inside and closing it behind him.

A beautiful woman was perched on the end of the bed, and as their eyes met, she smiled lazily. Dark blonde curls met her shoulders, and hazel – brown eyes rimmed with kohl and long dark eyelashes flashed at him. Her lips were soft and pink. Noah could see why she was Tom's woman of choice. She wore blue shorts and white t-shirt, which, in certain light, became transparent.

"Hi,' she stood, padded over to him on bare feet and held out a small hand, 'Noah, is it?"

He nodded, momentarily tongue tied, before enveloping her hand in his, "Yes, hi"

"Maria,' she took his coat, pulling it slowly off of his shoulders and hanging it on a hook on the back of the door, 'do you want to come and sit on the bed?"

Noah shrugged, finding that he was nervous for some reason, "Why not."

Maria studied him carefully. "You're not my usual type of client."

"What do you mean?"

"You don't seem like you would need the girlfriend experience."

There was a pause as Noah tried to decide how to respond, and Maria sat back with a satisfied smile on her face "You're a police officer aren't you?"

"I am' He decided that honesty would be best, and he found he was much more relaxed now that she knew, 'but I'm not here about the business."

"So why are you here?" She was curious now, curling her legs underneath herself.

"Tom Carol. He says that he was here on the night of a kidnapping. Can you confirm his last few bookings?"

Maria laughed then, "He comes every night."

"Every night? Why?"

"Lonely I guess. He alone pays my rent.' She smiled, 'He gets here at about nine p.m, and stays until seven a.m. The real girlfriend experience."

"Someone to come home to every night' Noah nodded; it was sad, but understandable he supposed. Especially with Maria, who seemed to epitomise the perfect, down-to-earth yet beautiful woman, 'how long has he been doing that for?"

Maria looked thoughtful for a moment, "Years. I came a year ago, but before that he had the girlfriend experience with somebody else. He says he prefers me though."

"Do you think that you can get me some sort of print out of all of Tom's appointments over the last month?"

Maria nodded, pulling some plimsolls onto her feet and heading out of the room.

When she had brought a file holding proof that Tom Carol had in fact spent every night for at least the last month here with Maria, Noah left, holding a hand up to the receptionist by way of goodbye, and strode to the car, slipping into his seat avoiding Ruth's laughing gaze.

"You were in there for a while Noah" She held back a grin as Noah shook his head.

"Tom sees a lady called Maria regularly, very regularly,' he pulled the booking schedule out of the file and passed them to her, 'every night in fact."

"The Girlfriend Experience" Ruth read.

"Yep, he arrives every night at nine, stays until seven"

"Wow' Ruth passed the paperwork back, and began to drive away, 'so he was definitely here that night."

"He was' Noah felt suddenly deflated as he realised what this meant, 'so now we have no suspects again, back to the drawing board."

*

Chapter Thirteen

Felicity barely noticed that she was at the hospital now. The smells, the sounds, the windowless rooms had all become familiar to her as though they were home.

She had been there for a few hours already, busying herself by rearranging the room, watering the new bunch of flowers that had appeared without a card, or indeed any sign of whoever had sent them, and throwing out old ones.

She had read to her mum for a bit, the book that she had just started when she had been attacked. She had hoped in some strange way that by continuing with it, her mother might have recognised it and woken up.

Now, she was sat beside her, holding her lifeless hand in both of her own warm ones, regaling her with the stories of the past few days.

"So, I'm not sure whether I'll even get into university now Mum. But I'm trying not to worry about it, there doesn't seem any point, considering.' She sighed, wishing that her mum could respond with one of her reassuring phrases, 'anyway, I have Ella, and Callum who has made quite the impression, despite not knowing him for long"

She felt her cheeks heat up, glad that her mother couldn't see her.

She was so busy thinking about Callum, that she didn't notice the first time that it had happened. Then it happened again, and she stared for a long moment, at the fingers that were resting upon her palm. They had moved, she knew that they had.

"Mum?" She whispered, holding her breath. This time she saw them as well as felt them, tapping twice against her palm.

Felicity stood sharply from her seat, jogging across the room and calling out through the door for a nurse. Excitement was making her jittery, and she paced the room, watching her mother carefully.

"What is it?" The nurse looked concerned and moved quickly to the bed, glancing between the monitor and Felicity for an explanation.

"She moved' Felicity told her, her words rushing out too quickly, 'her fingers moved, three times!"

"The nurse stopped, turning and looking at her seriously, "Are you sure?"

"Yes, I'm sure, I didn't imagine it."

"Ok,' Seemingly satisfied, the nurse began taking her mothers' blood pressure 'well in that case, I'll alert her doctor and he will arrange all necessary tests and scans to find out whether there are any significant changes."

"Thank you"

"Why don't you go home and relax Felicity, we'll call you once we have any results. The tests will take a good long while yet" The nurse smiled, and seeing that it was genuine, Felicity nodded, knowing that she would only go mad sitting around here.

As she practically ran along the corridor, she pulled out her phone, dialling and putting it to her ear, listening to the ringing with building excitement.

"Hello?" The voice sounded surprised, and Felicity froze for a moment.

She hadn't realised that she had called Noah; she must have dialled his number on impulse. She wasn't surprised, he was the first person that she wanted to tell, even if she hadn't intended to.

"Hi" it came out as a whisper so that she had to repeat it.

"Is everything ok?"

"Yes!' A tear slid from the corner of her eye as the happiness suddenly overwhelmed her, 'everything is great Noah. My mum moved!"

"That's great!" He sounded so genuinely happy that Felicity's heart swelled for a moment.

"I know! It was only her fingers, but still, it's been so long!"

"Why don't we celebrate?" He sounded so hopeful, that Felicity couldn't help but become enthused.

"Ok' she skipped, joy spreading right through to her toes, 'what will we do?"

"Leave it to me,' she could hear him smiling as he spoke, 'I'll be with you in ten."

Smiling to herself, she hung up, and wandered over to a bench just outside the hospital. It surrounded by rose bushes and lavender, and bees and butterflies buzzed and flapped around her. The sun was beating down, and suddenly she had never felt so lucky.

It had occurred to her that it might not be a good idea to spend time with Noah. She knew that she still liked him, if not loved him, and she couldn't stand the thought of Noah rejecting her. She was sure that he would be over her by now. Maybe he was even with Ruth. But she was so happy right now that she pushed the thought out of her mind – she didn't want anything to ruin this.

"Hey!"

Felicity started as Noah's voice broke through her cloud of thought. He was leaning out of his car door, grinning at her across the roof, and her heart skipped a beat. He looked exactly the same, but better somehow.

She skipped over to him, leaning her hands against the roof, she smiled back at him "Fancy seeing you here" She murmured, trying to appear casual.

"Need a lift anywhere?" Slipping back into his seat, Noah leaned over and opened her door.

She climbed into the car, and glanced at him, unable to keep the smile from her face "Sure, but I don't know where I'm heading. Surprise me?"

Noah nodded gravely, "I'll do my best".

*

"This is amazing" Felicity gazed in wonder at the view.

Noah had brought her to the moors, and they were currently perched upon the rocks of one of the Tors, with a rushed picnic of badly made sandwiches and supermarket chocolate bars. Plastic bottles of fizzy drinks had been opened, and though it wasn't quite the brilliantly organised picnic that Callum had arranged for them, somehow it felt better.

"I'm glad that you like it,' he took a mouthful of ham sandwich and chewed it thoughtfully, 'listen, I need to ask you something before I get too involved here"

Felicity swallowed, her heart racing, "Go ahead."

He turned away a little, his cheeks flushing pink, "That guy who was at your house the other morning?"

Felicity looked at him sideways before becoming very interested in a mark on her knee, "It's nothing serious. I don't really know what it is. I don't love him Noah."

She looked up at him now, wanting him to see that this was true, and wanting him to hear what she wasn't saying out loud.

"Are you seeing each other?"

"Not really. Not officially. We've hung out a couple of times, and yes I've kissed him."

Noah stood abruptly, anger clouding his face, "Right. Well. I didn't realise that it was so easy for some people to turn off their feelings."

Felicity stared at him for a moment, blinking in disbelief. "How dare you?! I didn't turn my feelings for you off at any moment, not for one second! But you didn't talk to me. And every time we have spoken you've been awkward, as if you wish I wasn't there. What did you want me to do Noah, wait for years until you've grown up enough to talk to me like an adult?"

They looked at each other, both breathing heavily, cheeks flushed with rage. The air felt colder now; despite the bright sun that was still beaming down at them, a fierce chilled wind was gusting around them, blowing Felicity's curls around her face, and forcing Noah to pull his jacket around himself.

Sadness filled her as she realised that the moment was gone, that moment that was going to bring them back together, or at least allow them to express themselves and bring about a bit of closure.

"Come on,' she whispered with melancholy, packing away the picnic, 'let's just go home, ok?"

"Fliss - "

She smiled at him sadly, "It's ok Noah, I don't think I can handle you apologising and letting me down gently.' She handed him his rucksack and headed toward his car, 'let's just go."

*

Chapter Fourteen

Lynette pushed the pile of crumbs around the plate and ignored her cold coffee, which appeared to have developed a skin. Her mum had gone home the day before, stating that her dad would probably be starved and down to his last pair of pants.

The house was so quiet without their little girl. No Disney princess films on the television, no trace of her sweet little voice and her tiny footsteps pattering against the floor. Her toys had been neatly placed in the toy cupboards for days now. What she wouldn't give for the usual higgledy-piggledy mess that followed her all over the place.

Matthew had been brilliant, staying in the house with her since her mum had left, making her copious hot drinks that she never started let alone finished, and trying to make sure she was eating. She felt guilty, because his child was missing too, but she couldn't seem to get herself out of this slump.

And he wasn't drinking now either, or at least not in front of her. He seemed to be functioning like a normal adult, she thought, trying to ignore the feeling that actually, a good stiff drink was what she needed.

She spent half of her time walking around like a zombie, or staring into space, and the other half sitting on Bella's bed, stroking the blankets and hugging her teddy bear. She'd probably be scared without it, she thought each time, which would spark a fresh wave of fear and horror to crash over her. What if she never got her back?

Now, she swept the crumbs off of the table and stood, closing her eyes and breathing deeply for a moment, pushing her flat palms against the rough wood.

She glanced up at the clock. Matthew had been out for nearly an hour, picking up some groceries, and she was starting to feel as though the loneliness was closing in around her. Already, they were becoming a tight unit again, depending upon each other. Although it did seem as if Lynette was far more dependent upon Matthew.

Wandering aimlessly into the hallway, trying not to look at the family photographs on the wall., she noticed that the pile of post, which she had left on the Welcome mat hours ago, had been placed neatly on the small oak table by the front door. Matthew must have picked it up, she thought.

Sighing, she threw the letters away, one by one, all being brown envelopes and unimportant to her for now. She paused. The final letter was in a small white envelope, and in printed letters written in blue biro, was her name. There was no address, no stamp. It had obviously been hand posted.

Her heart began to race, slamming against her ribs so that she thought it might burst out. With shaking hands, she peeled open the envelope and pulled out the sheet of paper, which had been folded into three.

LYNETTE,

IF YOU EVER WANT TO SEE BELLA AGAIN TELL THE POLICE TO STOP LOOKING. I WANT £5000 TRANSFERRED TO ME BY THE END OF THE WEEK. IF YOU AGREE, REPLY TO THIS MESSAGE BY PLACING YOUR ANSWER IN THIS ENVELOPE AND HIDING IT UNDER YOUR DOORMAT BY MIDNIGHT.

She began to hyperventilate. Maybe they hadn't hurt her, she told herself. But she didn't have five thousand pounds, especially not to spare, but not at all. She was living month to month as it was.

At that moment, Matthew crashed through the door, bags swinging from his arms.

"Goodness me Lynn, I nearly got you with that door then!" He exclaimed, panting, face puce with the effort.

"Matthew they've contacted us."

"What?!' He dropped the bags onto the floor, moving so that he could read the note over her shoulder, 'But Lynn, this is great, it means she's alive."

She shook her head, "No, it doesn't. It might be a trick. They might keep asking for money, and never give her back because she's dead' she stuffed the letter back into the envelope furiously, 'but even if she is alive Matthew, I don't have five thousand pounds! Do you?"

He rubbed a hand across his face, the hope falling from it, "No' He muttered resolutely, looking absolutely defeated, 'will we take this to the police?"

Lynette chewed her lip for a moment, tears pooling in her eyes. This felt so impossible. They had told them to stop the police, but what if that was a trick too?

"Yes' she nodded decisively. 'we will, it's the safest way."

*

Noah felt utterly depressed. Everything had gone wrong this afternoon. It was meant to be the moment that he and Felicity admitted their feelings and tried again. But he had well and truly blown it, he realised.

Had he expected her to wait? How could he? He shook his head. He had to forget about it now. She will probably see Callum again, and he was on duty tonight, he needed to concentrate.

He stared around at the evidence strewn across his desk, which didn't amount to much, he admitted, trying to ignore his phone ringing, until the officer on phone duty yelled at him across the office.

"Sorry,' he said immediately as he picked the call up, 'I'm just racking my brains over this kidnapping case."

"Well, I'd think of something, I've got the mother on the phone" He answered, putting the call through before Noah could respond.

"Officer Bennet?" Lynette's soft voice travelled along the phone lines to his ear as he strained to hear her.

"Yes, good evening Lynette, how are you?"

"Fine, fine, we've had a letter Officer."

He sat up, suddenly alert, "A letter? Handwritten?"

"Yes"

"And how many people have handled it since it came into the house?"

"Two, just myself and Matthew."

He nodded and then realised that they couldn't see him. "Ok Lynette, you need to put the letter down, and nobody touch it. If there are any prints left we want to be able to get them. I'll be over as soon as I can."

*

Now, as Noah drove away from Lynette and Matthew, he thought of how strange it was that he was suddenly staying there. After all, they had separated, and Matthew had been kept away from Bella. Why would Lynette want him there at all?

Although, he supposed that she needed any support that she could get in a situation like this.

They had sat, side by side, clutching each other's hands as though their lived depended on it.

He glanced at the letter which had been safely deposited in an evidence bag, and was now sitting on the passenger seat. Bella's life, at least, depended on it.

*

Felicity was holding the hand again, the one that had moved. Now, it was as still and lifeless as ever, but she refused to believe that nothing had changed. The doctor was on the opposite side of the bed with a young nurse, murmuring quietly as he demonstrated how to check her mothers' vital statistics.

Other than the low hum of their voices, and the steady beeping of the heart rate monitor, the room was completely silent.

Eventually, the doctor dismissed the nurse, who smiled shyly at Felicity as she went past, and dragged a chair over to where she was sitting. He was a very tall, thin man, and the chair was quite low, which made him look like a spider waiting to deliver bad news.

"How are you Miss. Lawrence?" He smiled kindly at her, and she wondered whether he was trying to placate her.

"I'm fine, and you can call me Felicity. I prefer it." She smiled back.

"Good' he nodded, leaning towards her with his sharp elbows against his bent knees, 'so your mums' fingers moved today, which of course is brilliant, absolutely what we are looking for."

He paused, and she stared back at him passively, waiting for the 'but' that she knew was coming.

"However, the brain scans, whilst they have shown a slight change which, again, is always a positive, there isn't enough of an improvement yet to guarantee or even speculate any kind of recovery."

"Ok, so what should I do. To help her." Felicity pushed away the disappointment, determined to help somehow.

"Well, I hear that you have been reading to her, talking to her. It may seem frustrating, but more of the same really. It's obviously done something."

When the doctor had left, and she was alone, she rested her forehead on her mums' stomach, closing her eyes and feeling the steady rise and fall of her breathing. She could almost forget that they were in a hospital.

She had known that it was too good to be true. The moment that things went wrong with Noah, she knew that it was a sign. She sighed, lifting her head, suddenly tired. It was late, and she still had to find a way home.

Kissing her mum on the forehead, she left, wandering slowly along the corridors, the lights beginning to dim behind her. Much like her heart, she thought, feeling it crack just a little.

*

Chapter Fifteen

Ruth stared at the letter through the glistening evidence bag, chewing her lip thoughtfully.

"Has it been analysed for prints?" She glanced at Noah, who was looking exhausted, head in his hands.

He nodded, "Nothing. Apart from the parents, but they both handled it when it arrived, so that's to be expected."

Ruth sighed, perching on the edge of Noah's desk. "Shall we talk to them again? The parents? See if they have had any revelations regarding possible enemies?"

Noah shook his head, trying to ignore the frustration welling up in his chest, "No, we've spoken to them enough for now. We'll just be wasting time,' he stared at his fingers thoughtfully, 'unless… unless we speak to Lynette alone?"

Ruth arched a brow, "So you suspect the dad?"

He chewed his lip. "There's just something that we're missing. And something off about him."

"I've been thinking it too' Ruth confirmed with a nod, 'I mean, he's been kept away from his own daughter for months and months. It's happened before, in other cases."

Noah shrugged, picking up the telephone handset, "I'll call her in to the station, it'll be much easier."

Ruth nodded as Noah punched the numbers into the phone. Listening to the monotonous ringing on the phone, he hoped that this was the beginning of the end of this case.

*

Felicity was curled into a miserable, self-pitying ball in her bed, the covers up to her chin despite the warmth when Ella arrived. She had forgotten that Ella had a key until she became bored of the doorbell being ignored and actually used it.

"Pathetic" She stated, hands on her hips as she frowned at her friend from the doorway.

"Shut up" Felicity mumbled, burrowing even further below the blankets.

"No!' Ella announced, striding across the room and pulling the blankets away with a sharp tug, 'I've just got you to a point where you're mildly happy and I'm not going to let you sink back into the cycle of misery!"

Felicity let out an exaggerated groan, wrapping a pillow over her head so that it covered her ears. She waited a few moments, surrounded by darkness, for Ella to drag her out again.

She heard a barely audible sigh, felt a weight pull the bed down by her legs.

"What happened Fliss?" Ella's voice was soft now, and she could feel the warmth of her beside her, and felt a little comfort.

"Noah.' She threw the pillow to one side, rolling onto her back so that she was staring up at the ceiling, 'we went for a picnic. It was a disaster."

"I'm sure it wasn't that bad." Ella tried.

"He just acted like a complete idiot El' she sat up now, anger bolstering her a little, 'he had seen me with Callum and he got so angry when I said we had kissed. It was as though he owns me, as though he hasn't avoided me all this time."

"So, if he is an idiot, why are you so upset about it?' Ella asked, flashing a half smile, 'he obviously isn't worth it."

Felicity returned the smile, though she didn't really feel it. Sometimes it was just easier to pretend that you agree, she thought.

*

When Lynette arrived at the station, she was ringing her hands, her eyes darting about the room as if she could gather any information that she needed in that one sweep. They hadn't given her any information over the phone, simply asked her to come in.

Noah noted that she had, surprisingly, come alone. Usually women like Lynette, women who had become nervous, arrived with a husband, or boyfriend. A male figure who made them feel safe. Maybe, he mused, she didn't really feel all that safe.

He pushed the thought out of his mind as he strode across the entrance hall to greet her, smiling warmly.

"Lynette, thank you for coming at such short notice."

"If it's to help my daughter, I'll go anywhere' her voice was shaking but she spoke fiercely, and Noah felt a fresh wave of sympathy for her, 'did you find something? With the letter?"

Noah pressed his lips together as he led her through the building to the questioning rooms. When they were safely inside, he shook his head regretfully.

"I'm sorry, no. The only prints that we could find were yours and your husbands.' He paused carefully, 'would you like a tea? Coffee? Water?"

She shook her head imperceptibly, watching her hands as if she had never seen anything so fascinating, and he indicated that she should take a seat opposite him.

He watched as she placed her hands flat on the table, attempting to control the shaking. Noah glanced up at the mirror behind her, knowing that Ruth was watching from the other side.

"You've asked me here to talk about my husband, haven't you?" She whispered, preoccupied by a knot in the table.

Noah sat back, excitement fizzing in his stomach. "What makes you say that?" He asked evenly.

"I don't think that he did it, if that's what you think" Her head snapped up to look at him, and it all came out in a rush.

"Did what, Lynette?"

"Well… anything. Whatever has happened to Bella,' she sagged against the desk, 'I just, I know how it might look."

"And how's that?"

"Well, you must know that he hasn't seen our daughter for a very long time."

Noah studied her. She was still nervous, but now that she had chosen to give her small speech, she was more defiant somehow. He nodded, in answer to her statement.

"Has he been in the house recently? In the days leading up to the kidnapping?"

Lynette shook her head, "No, the first time I saw him in months was after we reported her missing."

Noah knew that this appeared to be true; they hadn't found any evidence of his fingerprints or DNA in the house anywhere. Not even in Bella's room.

Swallowing his frustration, he stood, indicating that Lynette was free to go; "Thank you, I'm sorry if that was a waste of your time. We just have to cover everything, you know."

Her lips formed a small smile, "I understand."

After seeing Lynette to the front door, Noah made his way back to his office, where Ruth was waiting, pacing the floors impatiently.

"Well, that wasn't particularly helpful." She sighed, folding her arms.

*

Chapter Sixteen

Felicity awoke, panting and sweating, heart racing with visions of dark rooms, rope. Memories of screaming and fear and wanting to get away. Memories that aren't her own, and aren't even really memories yet.

And after a few beats of disorientation, she realised that she had been woken by the doorbell, which was dragging her back to reality. She stumbled from her bed, wrapping her arms against the sudden chill of clambering out from beneath the blanket, and tripped down the stairs, trying to make out the figure that she could see through the window.

After the dream that she had just had, she felt nerves rise like butterflies from her stomach. As Callum's smile became clear from the other side of the glass, Felicity swallowed those butterflies, feeling dizzy with relief, and then noticed her reflection, far too late to actually do anything about it.

"Hi" She yawned, pulling the door open and trying to summon a smile for him.

"Are you ok?" He wrapped his arms around her and she relished his warmth for a moment before stepping back into the house, indicating that he should follow.

"Oh, just, bad dreams…" She trailed off, half wanting to tell him all about it. But he wasn't from here, and he probably didn't know what everybody else did. She didn't think that it had gone any further than Devon. She just wanted one person who didn't see her as the crazy, psychic girl.

Callum raised a brow, sensing that she was holding back, and made his way to the kitchen.

"What are you doing?" She called out, following him curiously.

"Making you breakfast' he announced, 'you look awful, why don't you have a shower and get dressed, and food and coffee will be ready when you're done." He grinned to show that he was joking, but she went anyway, grateful to wash the dream off of her skin, and out of her hair.

"Ok,' she shouted, 'but I want the full works!"

She smiled at the sound of his laughter.

*

"Right' she announced decisively through a mouthful of mushroom, 'I'll tell you about my dream, but you can't laugh. This is a real thing."

He frowned, "I promise. No laughing."

"And you can't repeat this to anyone!"

He drew a cross over his chest and mimed poking his eye.

"I had a dream about the little girl that's missing. I could see… where she was. I could feel what she was feeling."

Callum stared at her passively, waiting for her to continue.

"But it was more like… what might happen in the future". She stopped here, watching him from the corner of her eye, waiting for his reaction.

After what felt like hours of silence, Callum turned to her seriously, "Well, have you spoken to the police?"

Felicity sat back surprised; she had expected more sarcasm, more disbelief.

"No, but I will. Maybe."

"You should' he insisted, 'you shouldn't deal with this all by yourself."

She thought about it as they finished their breakfast. She wanted to tell them. She would tell them, she decided. But she would still do a little investigating of her own.

*

Chapter Seventeen

"Oh god, not again!" Ella groaned, pacing her bedroom floor.

Felicity slumped back against her friends' bed, "Oh. So, you won't help me then?"

Ella sighed, dropping down next to her, "Well, of course I will.' She turned to her sharply, waving a finger at her, 'but I'll have you know I'm not happy about it!"

"Thank you!' Felicity grinned, hugging her tightly, 'I will speak to Noah too, just in case."

"That means that you actually have to talk to him" Ella pointed out with a smile.

Felicity rolled her eyes, feigning nonchalance. Inside, her heart skipped a beat. Things hadn't exactly ended well between them, and she didn't particularly want to see him again.

"You know' she began slowly, glancing slyly at Ella, 'I don't really think that we're in any danger from this person."

"Fliss!" Ella warned.

"We're not exactly the demographic, are we?' she insisted, leaning toward Ella as if it would convince her, 'the victim is a small child. We'll be fine."

"Yes, because anybody who ever chased after a kidnapper and possible killer came out well in the end, right?" Ella muttered, sarcasm dripping from every word.

"Look, I will go to him, if we need to.' Felicity pleaded, 'but we don't need to right now."

Ella glanced at her leg, where the scar was hidden by denim and bravado, and sighed loudly.

"Fine, but the minute, *the minute* it gets hairy, we go to Noah. Got it?!"

"Yes, got it' Felicity leaped to her feet, pulling a notebook and pen from her handbag, 'so, what do we know so far?"

"Nothing" Ella announced, helpfully, with a cheerful grin.

Felicity ignored her, beginning to pace the room, "We know that the parents are no longer together."

"Ok, well, do you want to talk to them?"

"I think that's the only way. It's all that we have for now.' She stopped, frowning at her notes, 'but what if they say something to Ruth and Noah? Namely Ruth."

"Look, can't we just go to the police? Come on, Fliss, we're all grown-ups."

"Speak for yourself."

*

"I can't believe that you talked me into this Fliss!" Ella whispered angrily, adjusting her black t-shirt, tucking it into her black jeans.

"Sssh!"

They were crouched in the bushes at the end of the path leading to Lynette Baker's front door, the door of the poor little girl who had disappeared.

"Come on." Felicity said decisively, straightening and making her way up the path. She wished that she was as confident as she was making herself appear. The sky was almost black, and fog-filled, the moon only just visible above the houses. She was feeling more than a little nervy as the front door grew bigger before them.

"Hey!"

The voice was deep, clouded by confusion. Felicity and Ella squinted into the rapidly descending darkness.

The front door opened, suddenly wide and a flood of light streamed onto the path.

"Who are you?" Matt took a step towards them, frowning.

"Um, my name is Felicity, Mr. Baker, and this is Ella' she moved cautiously towards him, 'I'm here to talk to you about your daughter."

"Are you with the police? We usually have Ruth and Noah."

"Not exactly,' she paused, attempting to find the right words, 'I... see things. I solved the murder that happened here a few months back? I've had some... visions that I think are relevant to your daughters kidnapping."

Matt was silent for a long moment, and a cloud passed over the moon, blanketing his face in a stormy black. In that moment, Felicity's stomach clenched, and a wave of nausea that told her that this was a mistake rose to her chest.

Slowly, he stepped from the doorway, shoes silent against the concrete somehow, as if he were floating. His eyes blazed, and his mouth was twisted in anger. He walked until he was inches from her face, and she could feel his hot breath against her cheek. Ella's hand shot out from behind her, wrapping her fingers around Felicity's own.

"My daughter is none of your business!' he spat venomously, his voice a harsh hiss, 'don't you ever come near this house ever again! Get away. NOW!"

For a moment they were frozen, Matt breathing heavily into the air between them.

"Fliss' Ella whispered shakily, pulling on her hand, 'please, let's just go."

Felicity glanced at Matt's clenched fists and allowed herself to be tugged away from him and down the path.

"Hey!' she called, turning as they reached the street. She watched the figure of him stop and angle slightly to face them over his shoulder, 'what are you so afraid of?"

For a horrible, stomach sickening moment, it seemed as though he would come after them, and then he disappeared, back into the brightness of the house.

Felicity took a deep breath, wrapping her arms around herself, suddenly chilled to the bone despite the summer heat of the night.

*

"I did something stupid." Felicity let it all out in a rush, so that nobody had the chance to say hello.

"Are you ok?" Noah asked, concern breaking through.

She sighed, preparing herself for another fight, "I may have gone to speak to Bella's family." A drawn-out silence crackled across the line between them, and Felicity could only assume that Noah was trying very hard not to lose his temper.

"Fliss, I know that you mean well, but Lynette Baker is in a very vulnerable state right now."

"Well, you'll be pleased to know that we were headed off by Mr. Baker.' She murmured drily, 'I have to say Noah, I know that this is a difficult time for them, but he didn't seem so much upset as angry."

"Why, what did he say?"

"He said that his daughter was none of our business and they we are never to come near that house every again. He was like a dragon, he was livid!"

"His child is missing Fliss, he probably doesn't want to be badgered by strange girls on his doorstep." Noah reasoned, and Felicity suddenly felt an irrational need to hang up on him.

"No, you didn't see him Noah' she leaned her forehead against her bedroom window, staring at the inky black outside and felt a shiver run down her spine, 'I'd keep an eye on him.

*

Chapter Eighteen

"Officer Bennett, there is a Matt Baker here for you?" The voice sounded tinny and far away as it travelled through the phone line, and Noah found himself wishing that he really was far away.

"Send him in please" Noah responded wearily.

"I got this" Matt announced, pushing into the room and slamming a wrinkled piece of paper onto the desk.

"What's 'this'" Noah asked, leaning over to see it.

On the desk lay a photograph. It was a candid shot of the profile of a small girl. A small girl bearing a strong resemblance to Bella Baker. She took up most of the photograph, but Noah pulled on a pair of gloves to bring the picture closer to his face, and study what little he could see of the background.

"You don't know where this has come from?" He urged, squinting as if that could help him have a clearer view.

"Of course, I don't know where it came from!" Matt growled. He looked weary and tired, eyes blood shot.

Instinctively, Noah tried to edge subtly closer to Matt; he suspected that he had been drinking. There was a mildly sour smell, blowing at him as Matt breathed.

"Have you been drinking Mr. Baker?"

Matt drew back, a look of petulance passing over his face, "How dare you! And so what if I have, my daughter is missing for gods sakes!"

Noah held his hands up in front of him, "Ok, sorry. It's your prerogative, I'm sure I would be the same' he turned back to the letter, 'leave this with me, we'll get it analysed and I'll be in touch."

Matt nodded, avoiding Noah's eyes and leaving silently, closing the door carefully behind him.

He stared at the profile of Bella Baker, thinking about her parents, their relationship and, namely, her father. Felicity was right, something was off with him.

*

Ruth watched him thoughtfully for a moment before nodding.

"I'll find out whether we can have someone watching the house for the next twenty-four hours.' She promised, jotting it down on a post it note, 'I hope we find her soon."

Noah swallowed the bubble of fear that had formed in his throat, "Do you think-' he paused, briefly closing his eyes, 'you know, if we do find her now she's probably…"

He trailed off, not wanting to say the word that he had been thinking of.

"Right,' Ruth scraped back her chair, avoiding his gaze, and made her way to the door of her office, 'let's get a lookout stationed, and see what else we can come up with."

Noah followed, trying to match the false confidence that his partner was exuding, but all that he could think about was the thought that he didn't dare fully form. And the result that he knew to be statistically true.

He sighed as Ruth pushed the front door open, bright light flooding in at them, a misrepresentation of everything that they were feeling right about now.

*

Felicity knew that, in most cases, if the missing child wasn't found within twenty-four hours, the outcome was less likely to be a positive one. She shook her head; it wouldn't do her any good to dwell on it.

"Mum, can you just wake up now' she whispered, resting her head gently against her mothers' chest, 'I don't know if I can do all of this again. Especially not without you cooking me your awful food as comfort."

She allowed herself a soft chuckle, before closing her eyes against the tears that had sprung unexpectedly into her eyes. Maybe Ella was right; maybe they should never have started this in the first place. It didn't exactly turn out well the first time they decided to play Nancy Drew.

But maybe she had been given this ability for a reason. She couldn't imagine how she would feel if she just ignored them, and didn't try to find Bella.

"What do you think Mum?' she asked, lifting her head and watching her peaceful face for any reaction, 'should I just forget about it?"

"I'll take your silence as encouragement" Felicity stated, hugging her, already knowing that she would carry on anyway.

*

Chapter Nineteen

"We saw some very interesting things last night." Officer Smith announced, sweeping into the room, and dropping some photographs onto the desk.

Matt Baker, leaving the house at one a.m, with a bundle in his arms, arriving back at three a.m, empty handed and exhausted.

"Where was he going?" Noah demanded.

"We followed him, and he was going back to his house."

Noah felt disappointment sink into his stomach, "Oh. Well, we've already been to his house."

"But did you search it?"

Noah grinned as a jolt of excitement coursed through him. "See if you can arrange a warrant for us, Smith? Please. Let me know as soon as you've got it, you can accompany myself and Ruth there.' He raised a brow, 'just in case."

Officer Smith nodded, with the enthusiasm of somebody new to the job. He didn't know about the aftermath of dealing with evil, murderers and kidnappers, Noah thought, grimly.

He shook his head. He was only twenty-one, had only been a police officer for a matter of months; how did he become so negative?!

"Did anything happen last night?' Ruth poked her head in, 'I saw Smith leaving."

Noah sighed inwardly, spreading the photographs across the desk; "Matt left Lynette's house at one a.m with something in his arms. He returned to his own home, and then left there, returning to Lynette at three a.m."

"Have you requested a warrant?"

"Smith's on it" Noah nodded.

"Shall we speak to Lynette again? See whether she knows anything about Matt leaving?"

"Actually, yes, great idea.' He pushed the pictures haphazardly into the file and stood, 'shall we?"

*

"Fliss?" Ella's voice travelled faintly down the phone lines to Felicity's ear. Felicity pushed her face into her warm pillow and groaned.

"What do you want at this ungodly hour?"

"I'm assuming that you haven't seen the local paper this morning?" She asked hesitantly.

"Why, have they found her? Did they find Bella?" Felicity threw the blankets off of her sticky legs, and began to run down the stairs to the waiting newspaper at the bottom.

"No, no they haven't, but – maybe you should wait until I'm there before you read it?"

"Why' Felicity laughed, unfurling the newspaper, 'Oh my god!"

Her own face was staring out from the front page, right there in black and white, along with a tiny photograph of Bella.

" 'Eighteen year old local psychic sees kidnapped child Bella Baker in her dreams',' She read the headline, hands shaking, ' 'an anonymous source says that Felicity Lawrence has seen where Bella is being held.' Ella that's not true! I could see little bits, but this makes it sound as though I know exactly where she is!"

"It's not that bad" Ella responded hesitantly.

"Yes, it is' Felicity snapped, throwing the newspaper down onto the breakfast bar with a slap, 'it's awful! If the parents see this, they'll think that Bella's been found. I need to call Noah, I'll speak to you later."

*

"Have you seen the newspaper?" Felicity asked, feeling sick as she heard herself echo Ella's words.

"Of course I have' Noah hissed, clearly struggling to keep the irritation out of his voice, 'we've all seen it. Ruth and I are in big trouble."

"I'm sorry!' She dropped her head into her hands, 'I didn't go to the papers, I swear I didn't. All I did was tell Callum about a dream I had,"

Noah let out a burst of air into her ear, "Well, if you've seen where she is then why didn't you come to me?!"

"Because I haven't seen where she is Noah, I promise. Callum's twisted it to make it more... exciting I suppose."

There was a long pause, and for a moment Felicity wondered whether Noah had hung up on her.

Eventually he said, "Well, regardless Fliss, the parents have seen this. Do you know how this must feel to them."

"I'm sorry" She whispered, trying her best not to cry.

"Look, I know you didn't mean for this to happen' Noah's voice was gentle now, but weary, 'but I really have to go. Damage control."

Felicity listened as the call clicked to signal it's end, and stared at the silent phone. She didn't know what to do to fix this, she realised. Callum had ruined everything; their friendship, Noah and Ruth's reputations, and more importantly, the Bakers'. For a short while, they had believed that they would soon have their little girl back with them. And then that hope was ripped away from them.

Anger flooded through her, leaving an acidic pool in her stomach.

*

Chapter Twenty

"First of all, Mrs. Baker, I want to apologise for the article in the newspaper this morning' Ruth said, following her into the living room, 'we have spoken with Miss. Lawrence this morning and she is also very apologetic. It seems that she decided to put her trust in the wrong person"

Lynette swiped roughly at a tear and smiled shakily, "It's ok"

"Is your husband at home Mrs. Baker?" Noah asked mildly.

"No, he's gone out to do some grocery shopping' she looked at them, her eyes flicking between the two, dark with confusion, 'is everything ok?"

Noah indicated that they should sit down before continuing, "Have you noticed anything strange about Mr. Baker's behaviour?"

"I thought that I had already answered questions about Matt?" Her cheeks flushed with annoyance.

"Mrs. Baker, your husband has been seen sneaking out of the house to return to his own home between one in the morning and three in the morning' Ruth leaned towards her almost conspiratorially, 'if that was my husband, I'd be a little… suspicious."

Lynette stared at her hands for a moment, before lifting her gaze to Ruth, tears swimming in her eyes. A million emotions seemed to pass over her face in the space of seconds, but suspicion won out.

"Well… what does he do? When he's at his house?" She asked hesitantly.

"We don't know' Noah said, shrugging, 'we don't have permission to go in there. Not unless you have any more information for us."

Lynette squeezed her eyes closed as though shutting everything out, "Well… he has been quite unstable recently' her voice was soft and trembling, 'before this I mean."

"Unstable how?"

"Well, he'd lost his job, he was drinking a lot. I didn't want Bella or myself around that anymore, so we left. I didn't want to leave Bella alone with him, sometimes he would pass out for hours' she glanced up then, guilt splashed across her face, 'it was for her safety. But he kept coming at all hours trying to get to her."

She watched as Ruth scribbled the details into a notebook, and leaned forward desperately.

"But I really don't think that he would do something like this." Lynette's face crumpled.

Ruth put her hand over Lynette's, "Lynette, I know that this is difficult, and of course, Matt is probably innocent. But we need to rule that out."

Lynette nodded miserably.

"We need you to keep an eye on him, and give us a call as soon as he leaves the house.' Noah instructed, 'we'll have some undercover officers outside who will follow him, and we'll meet them there."

Ruth smiled at Lynette, "Once it's done, we can stop focusing on your husband."

"Promise?"

"I promise."

*

"Well, Callum's gone" Felicity sighed, shoving the straw into her mouth and taking a large slurp.

"What do you mean gone?" Ella stared at her in disbelief.

"Apparently, he's gone back home early' she shook her head, and murmured sarcastically, 'I wonder why."

"I just can't believe that he would do that.' Ella glanced over to the counter, 'does his uncle know?"

Felicity nodded, "He said that he was sorry. To be honest, I wouldn't be surprised if he was the one who had sent Callum home."

"How did Noah react?"

Felicity rolled her eyes, "Not great. But he didn't act as though he completely hates me, which is an improvement on recent relations."

Ella laughed, "He'll come around, I know it. You're perfect for each other."

"How can I know that?' Felicity looked pained, 'we haven't even kissed!"

"But it's different with the two of you' Ella insisted, 'it's just… different."

Felicity shrugged, flashing her a small smile. Maybe they were. Maybe they weren't.

At the moment, it felt as though they would never even be friends again.

*

Two Years Ago

Shaking, he stood for a moment, staring at the door, which had bounced away from the door frame. Slowly, he turned, a strange buzzing beginning to fill his ears.

As he moved towards his desk, each step was heavy, as though he were walking through treacle. He looked around at his workstation, everything that he had built up over the last ten years of his life. None of it mattered now. Stuffing the photograph of his wife and his three-year-old daughter into his bag, he pushes away from the cold surface of the desk, takes a deep breath and moves quickly across the office floor.

Nobody says anything, nobody even looks at him, he notices bitterly.

*

"Daddy's home!' he can hear Lynette's voice floating from the kitchen as he closes the door softly behind him, 'he's early isn't he?"

He can hear the questioning lilt in her voice, and his mouth fills with saliva as though he might be sick.

"Daddy!" his beautiful, blonde-haired little girl sprints towards him, throwing herself into his arms.

"Hello little one' he drops a gentle kiss upon her head before flashing a smile at his wife, 'hi"

"Hi' she stands before him, leaning against the breakfast bar and watching him with concern, 'what's wrong?"

He shakes his head and lets out a barely audible laugh, "You know me too well' placing Bella carefully onto the kitchen floor, he sits, indicating that Lynette should do the same, 'I've been made redundant"

Lynette watches him for a moment, worry flitting across her face for a very short moment, before wrapping her arms around him carefully, "It's ok. We'll be ok. You'll get something else."

He smiled into her shoulder. How lucky he was.

*

Chapter Twenty-One

Noah stared at the clock, watching the hands move at minus speed around the face. They were waiting, rather impatiently, for the call, the one that would say that Matt Baker was on the move.

He was sure now that Matt had something to do with it. It was always the father, he thought to himself.

"How are you holding up?" Ruth asked, pulling a chair up beside him.

"Tired,' he replied with a half-smile, 'so pretty much the same as usual."

Ruth chuckled, resting her head on the back of her chair and closing her eyes, "God, I hope that we get him. This may be a long night!"

*

Matt Baker, exhausted and beginning to feel a little bit scared of what he was doing, hovered in the doorway of the spare room, listening intently for any sign that Lynette was nearby.

When he was satisfied that he had the time that he needed, he rushed back into the room, closing the door firmly behind him. As an afterthought, he locked it.

Moving further into the room, he pulled open the doors of the old wooden wardrobe, and reached to the back of a shelf at the top. He pulled out first a bag, and then cereal bars, bags of crisps and dried fruit. After feeling around a little more, pulling himself up onto the tips of his toes, he dragged two bottles of water down, throwing everything into the bag.

Quickly, he shoved the bag back onto the shelf, closing the cupboard door firmly upon his deceit.

*

Lynette chewed the skin around her fingernails, wincing as she came too close to the cuticle. She jumped as she heard Matt's footsteps descending the stairs, and chastised herself silently; if she was going to get away with this, she was going to have to stop being so nervous.

She had been listening to him moving around up there, wondering what he was doing, and she hated it. Despite everything, he had been there for her during all of this, and she couldn't stand the thought that it had all been an act.

She smiled as naturally as she could as Matt stepped into the room, cheeks red with exertion, and panting a little.

"Hi" He raised his hand in a strange, small wave, fingers shaking a little, and Lynette realised that he was nervous. Why was he nervous?

She mentally shook her head, it was just the pressure of the whole situation, they were all like it. On edge.

"You ok?" She asked, throat feeling dry and constricted.

"Yes, yeah, just, you know." He rubbed a hand across his face, and Lynette felt a rush of sympathy for him.

Eighteen Months Ago

Opening one eye, he peers about himself, trying to swallow the acidic nausea that is rising from his chest. He groans. Lynette is gone, and the house is silent.

Ignoring the layer of sweat across his skin, he glances at the clock beside him. Lunchtime. Lynette and Bella have been gone for a couple of hours.

Hauling himself out of bed, he rubs his eyes and forces himself to move through the deep-seated ache in his muscles.

On the dining room table, the job section of the newspaper had been pointedly laid out, several red circles visible from the door way. His heart plummeted into his stomach. He couldn't do it anymore. Every interview that he had been to in the last six months, and truthfully there hadn't been many to go to, had fallen flat. There is just too much competition, a lot of it being his previous workmates.

Feeling the stress bubble in his stomach, he rips open the fridge desperately. She had emptied it. He pressed his nails into his palms trying to dispel the rising panic. The panic which was currently, always, battling with self-loathing to take centre stage.

Scrabbling underneath the kitchen sink, he feels his finger-tips brush against the warm crushed plastic of an old, half-empty cider bottle. He hugs it to himself for a moment before raising it to his lips with shaking hands and sipping gratefully. The taste was sour and foul, and yet he felt his heart slow to a normal rhythm, and the heat fade from his face as the alcohol spread through his body.

He was surprised that she hadn't found this one. Weekly, Lynette would clear the house of alcohol, somehow seeking out all of his hiding places. At the thought of her, and of their child, his head filled with a cloud of despair.

He gulped down the last of the cider, tears running rivers down his cheeks.

*

Chapter Twenty-Two

Felicity stared up at the door of the police station looming above her, and took a deep breath. She was going to fix things with Noah once and for all. Maybe they could work together on the case.

She listened to the slapping of her plimsolls against the stone steps, trying to calm herself. She didn't know why she was so nervous. It was Noah for God's sakes!

"Fliss?"

She glanced up, startled, allowing the door to swing to a noisy close behind her. Noah was at the coffee machine near the front desk, brows furrowed with confusion, and she moved towards him, breathing deeply.

"Hi Noah"

"What are you doing here?"

Felicity felt her heart sink, "I'm sorry. For everything' she peered up at him, trying to smile, 'not just the article, although of course for that. But for avoiding you. Especially when I needed you."

Noah watched her, a slow smile spreading across his face as her cheeks grew pink, before taking a step towards her and enfolding her in his arms.

"I'm sorry too' he spoke into her hair, 'I've missed you Felicity Lawrence."

She looked up at him, grinning, chin resting on his chest. His eyes sparkled into hers, and her stomach ached with a longing that she hadn't felt before.

"I've missed you too Noah Bennett" She reached up onto her toes, so that she could feel his breath on her cheek.

"Noah!' Ruth's voice cut in between them so that they jumped apart as suddenly as they had come together, 'she's called! We need to go!"

*

Lynette placed the phone back into its' receiver, hands shaking. She was tired, so, so tired, but she had forced herself to stay awake, peeling her eyelids apart each time they attempted to close.

At about twelve thirty, a bang, followed by hushed muttering, startled her. She lay completely still, eyes wide. She could hear everything now, she was so alert. She was sure that she could hear her blood moving through her veins.

A few moments after she had heard that first sound, she realised that footsteps were approaching her room, almost completely silent, and she squeezed her eyes shut, wondering when he had got so sneaky.

She tried her best to remain immobile as a sudden breeze rushed in at her with the opening of the door, and then back past her again as it closed. She waited for five minutes, before moving quickly to the window, peering through a crack in the curtains.

She watched as Matt moved swiftly down the garden path to his car, peering around him, a duffle bag in hand. She watched still as he clambered in, and drove away, the rumble of is engine low in the silence.

With a sob catching in her throat, she had found Ruth's card and snatched up the phone.

Now, she sat upright in bed, wondering just who she had married.

*

Twelve Months Ago

"No, please, Lynette. Please don't do this!" He forced himself to speak clearly, fighting against his tongue which seemed to have fallen asleep.

Lynette pushed past him, throwing the last of his bags onto the path outside. Her voice was shaking, and her lashes were wet, "I can't have you here anymore!' she turned to him, her face a strange combination of anger, fear and a deep sadness, 'you don't see Bella's face when she finds you, passed out on the sofa. When she tries to wake you up and you won't!"

His heart constricted at the thought of his poor daughter, confused and scared as he lay unresponsive.

"I can change' he grabbed her arm, and she pulled it sharply away in disgust, 'please Lyn!"

"No!"

They stared at each other for a moment, both of them with elastic bands so tight around their chests that they couldn't breathe. He wasn't sure whether he was having a heart attack, he was in so much pain.

"Daddy?" They broke eye contact at the sound of Bella's quiet little voice, her sweet little face peering up at them, confused, brows knitted.

Realising that he had no choice, he knelt down until he was at eye-level with her, and flashed her a watery smile, "Daddy has to go baby girl' he felt his voice catch, and cleared his throat, 'Daddy will be with Nanny and Grandad, and you can visit whenever you want to, ok?"

"But I don't want you to!" She threw her arms around his neck, burying her face in the crook.

"I have to" He peeled her body away from him, and he felt as though his soul were being ripped from his body. Blinking away the tears so that she wouldn't see him crying, he kissed her forehead softly and, on shaking legs, made his way to the front door.

Amongst the bags of clothes, he turned one last time to look at the place that he called home, the people that he called family watching him, sombre, from the doorway.

And then the door closed upon him.

*

Chapter Twenty-Three

"Let me come with you!" Felicity insisted, following Noah and Ruth out to the patrol car.

"No" Noah spoke firmly, as Ruth glanced at her, eyes flashing with frustration.

"I can help."

They stopped, so that Felicity almost knocked into the back of Ruth. Ruth and Noah glanced at each other.

"Noah…" Ruth warned, though without much conviction.

"Fine' Noah narrowed his eyes at Felicity, 'but Ella is not coming!"

Ten minutes later, having picked Ella up from the pub where she had been patiently waiting for Felicity to arrive with gossip, they were driving swiftly and deftly towards Matt Baker's home.

"When we get there, Ruth, you go in the front door, I'll go in the back' Noah spoke quickly, 'the two undercover officers will be waiting as back up, and they'll follow us in."

"What about us?" Ella grinned, the excitement palpable.

"You and Felicity will stay in the car and keep watch."

Ella and Felicity glanced at each other, raising eyebrows and shaking heads.

"I didn't come here to sit and watch' Ella said, crossing her arms over her chest, 'that's just something that you've made up to keep us out of the action!"

"No' Ruth replied in a mildly mocking tone, 'it's really important."

Ella rolled her eyes, sitting back in her seat with a purposefully loud sigh.

*

Matt stood in the centre of the dark sitting room, breathing deeply for a few moments. He didn't want to do this anymore; he wished he could take it all back. Maybe they should leave. He and Bella, just fly away to a different country. Maybe they should have done that to start with. He pushed a hand through his hair, before heading to the hallway and opening a door carefully.

He stared down into the darkness, just able to make out the first step down into the basement. He placed his foot gently onto it, wincing as it creaked, though there was nobody else here, so he didn't need to be quiet.

*

Six Months Ago

He knew that he shouldn't be there. But he hadn't seen her for five months. It hadn't taken long for Lynette to push him out of Bella's life completely. He would arrange to pick her up, or for Lynette to bring Bella to him, but his wife, or ex-wife, always cancelled at the last minute.

For every day that Lynette kept he and his daughter apart, his dependence on alcohol grew, almost as though he was trying to replace Bella with the sweetly bitter taste of… anything that he could get his hands on.

Now, he stood at the end of the path, staring at the front door, wondering what would happen if he knocked on it.

The living room was dark, and the light from the television pulsed, casting a warm glow through the window. He could see the shadows of them moving against the curtain.

And then suddenly Bella's face was up at the window, framed by the chiffon. She was laughing at something. She hadn't seen him, and after a few moments she disappeared; the drawing of the curtains seemed so final, that he felt that his heart was breaking into a million pieces.

*

Chapter Twenty-Four

Noah and Ruth moved soundlessly through the house, guns in hands. As they met in the archway between the kitchen and the sitting room, they nodded to each other, heading for the stairs.

Making their way up, they split off again, heading for different bedrooms, silently opening wardrobes and peering under beds.

They emerged, full of confusion, frowning at each other. Where was he?

*

"Well, this isn't what I expected." Ella muttered, forehead pressed against the cool window.

"Me neither' Felicity replied, sitting upright and peering out at the house, 'El, is that a door?"

Felicity pointed through the darkness to a shadowy shape. Glancing at each other with guilty smiles, they quietly pushed open the car door, heading towards it with racing hearts.

The closer they came, the darker the shadows, and so Felicity pressed her hands against the wood until she came to a cold, metal handle and gasped triumphantly.

"Shall we go in?" She whispered, ignoring the nausea that had begun to rise in her throat.

Ella rolled her eyes, pushing open the door with a flourish. A slice of light was coming down at them, and they could just make out some stair leading up towards it.

Taking a simultaneous deep breath, they began to climb, shoes squeaking against the steps.

As the light grew closer, a soft murmuring began to reach their ears, and they paused for a moment to gain their courage.

Climbing the final few steps, they slowly opened another wooden door. On the other side, a small girl with long blonde hair was curled up on a bed, hungrily pushing crisps into her mouth. She wore a dirty pair of pyjamas. Beside the bed was a bucket, and Felicity couldn't help but feel appalled.

Matt Baker, dishevelled and smiling wearily, was crouched in front of her, clutching a bottle of water.

"Hey!"

*

Three Months Ago

She was nervous, he realised through the fog in his brain. She pushed her glasses back up her nose with shaking fingers, and looked at him with sympathy.

"I-I'm sorry, sir, Mrs. Adams has made it very clear that we mustn't let you onto school grounds,' she frowned, 'you shouldn't even be in the playground!"

"Please' he tried to blink away the tears, not wanting to appear unstable, 'please, I'm trying so hard. I'm not drinking, not even one little sip"

She chewed her lip, the sympathy obvious in her eyes.

"I can't, Mr. Baker, I'm sorry." She turned then, walking quickly away from him, the nerves palpable from across the playground.

Matt's heart began to race, almost too fast, and sweat sprang out on his forehead. He tried to remember where Bella's classroom was, how he could get to her from here.

Taking a deep breath, he ran, taking off past the student teacher who had denied him access, and was now staring at him open mouthed. He forced his way through the large double doors, ignoring the shouts of the receptionist, and racing down the corridor to the classroom that he remembered as hers.

His ribs hurt from the hammering of his heart, as he approached the classroom door. He pushed it open so that it swung away from him, hitting the wall and bouncing back.

A group of twenty small children stared at him, fear etched upon their little faces.

Not one of them was Bella.

*

Chapter Twenty-Five

Noah's head snapped up at the sound of Felicity's voice ringing through the house.

"Basement!" One of the back-up officers shouted up at them.

Noah swore under his breath, taking off down the stairs two at a time. Sprinting to the door, he kicked it so that it flew open, crashing into the wall; he shouldered through it, barely registering the rumble of footsteps following him down there.

Matt had his arm across his daughters' neck, a small knife in his hand. Felicity and Ella, faces pale, were across from them, arms outstretched, attempting to calm him down.

"I can't live without my little girl' he sobbed, tears tracking streaks along his cheeks, 'shoot me for all I care, I'll take her with me!"

Noah and Ruth edged forwards, guns outstretched, and Matt squeaked, tightening his grip and bringing the knife a little closer to Bella's throat. Bella let out a sob, which made Matt's face crumble.

"You don't want to kill her Matt' Felicity was breathless, as though she had been holding her breath for a long time, 'she's your baby girl. You love her more than anything, don't you?"

Matt nodded, a tear falling to the ground, leaving a dark patch on the grey concrete.

"Just let her go, let her go now, and everything will be ok. Don't you think that she deserves that?"

Felicity and Ella were moving subtly closer, and Matt wasn't seeing anything through his grief and tears.

"It's not fair' he whispered, his grip on Bella loosening a little, 'she's my baby. I know that I've been struggling but, I would never hurt her."

"Of course you wouldn't' Felicity soothed, so close now that she could touch the little girl, 'and we'll get you all the help that you need with this."

Matt let out another racking sob, and suddenly both Ella and Felicity plunged forwards; Ella ripping the knife from his hand, Felicity grabbing Bella around the waist and yanking her towards her.

Noah and Ruth rushed towards them, taking hold of Noah, and clapping cuffs around his wrists. He hung limply from them, quietly crying.

*

Epilogue

Felicity closed her eyes, breathing in the scent of the familiar and safe. It had been a week since Bella and Lynette had been reunited in a tearful and joyous occasion.

Her mum was still unconscious, but she was still sure that she had moved, that things were improving.

Just the previous morning, an envelope had dropped onto her doormat – she had passed her exam, and made it into university. A sense of relief mingled with fear flooded into her chest every time she thought about it.

And she was tired. She yawned, stretching her arms above her head, pulling the pillow around her to block out any sound. She paused. Something had brushed her hand.

Curling her fingers around it, she pulled out a scrap of paper, and unfurled it with mild interest.

I'm sorry.

*

Enjoy An Extract of Book One Of The Felicity Lawrence Series: Murder At First Sight.

Murder At First Sight

An extract of book one in The Felicity Lawrence Series

Prologue

Something glints as the sunlight slices through a gap somewhere in front of her. As she peers closer she realises what she is seeing. A knife. Her heart begins to pound and she can't seem to draw in enough air.

She tries to move, to reach for the blade, but her arms are trapped behind her back, and she gasps as thick rope grazes her wrists. Closing her eyes for a moment, she takes a deep, shaking breath before squinting into the darkness, attempting to make out shapes in the room.

Okay, she thinks, beams, I think I see beams! And hay. I'm smelling hay. Her eyes begin to dart about the room as she struggles to her knees. As her eyes adjust to the darkness, she blinks rapidly. A tractor is about five feet away.

A door. She shuffles toward the light. It's coming through the crack in the doors. Her breathing quickens as she realises that she can get out.

Desperately, she shuffles across the rough, gritty floor, sweat breaking out across her body. The knife is beside her now and she leans down as though to grab it between her teeth. She frowns as her distorted reflection swims in the surface of the knife; the person peering back at her does so with dark brown eyes which are wide with terror. Bright blonde hair frames her small face.

Suddenly, a slow creak sounds behind her and she whips her head around in terror.

"H- hello?" It comes out as a trembling whisper. Silence.

And then, out of the blue, something hard and cold jabs against her temple. A whimper slips out, though she is frozen in place, her galloping heart sending her dizzy.

It was as though it played out in slow motion; a bang, a searing pain as she felt her temple rip apart, and then, as she drifted away, an echoing ring, which faded in time with her.

*

It was still dark as Felicity Lawrence's eyes sprang open. Sweat ran down her neck and she rubbed it away. She glanced at the flashing numbers on her alarm clock. 4.49 am.

She stared up at the ceiling, waiting for her breathing to regulate. Turning her head slowly, she peered into the mirror next to the bed in curiosity. She still had her dark, wild curls and green eyes.

The dream had been so real; she could still smell the hay now. Tentatively, she rubbed at her temple.

Laying back against the pillow, Felicity swallowed her discomfort and squeezed her eyes closed.

It was just a dream, she told herself, as sleep engulfed her once more.

Chapter One

One Week Later

Glancing at her watch, she sighed, and peered down the empty street. The bus was late *again*. Frowning, Felicity tried to work out whether she would make it on time if she walked. She rolled her eyes and looked down at her brand new school shoes, which were rubbing blisters onto her toes already.

She began walking, firing off a quick text to her best friend Ella, before dialling the school office. The answerphone picked up, "Good Morning, this is Felicity Lawrence, I am on my way but I might be late, the bus-" she stopped abruptly as she rounded the corner and became faced with several police cars and an ambulance.

She shoved her phone into her bag looked around to see where she was exactly. The Anderson Farm. Now not actually owned by The Anderson's, or anybody at all in fact. It had been abandoned for about ten years, ever since the owner died with no surviving family to be found. She frowned. She felt a strange sense of déjà vu as she gazed at the large barn across the field. She could see people in large white suits and masks moving through a broken window at the top. A man and a woman in smart business wear were standing at the doors wearing gloves.

"Can I help you, miss?" She jumped at the unexpected voice and peered up at a young man, wearing a police uniform.

"Oh, no, s-sorry,' she watched him turn away before changing her mind, 'actually, Officer, can I just ask, what exactly happened here?"

He stared at her for a moment, before appearing to decide that she was trustworthy enough. He lifted his hat from his sandy blonde hair and ran his wrist across his forehead. She watched a bead of sweat trickle down his cheek and into his light smattering of stubble. He opened his top button and she silently thanked Mother Nature for the thirty degree heat.

"A young lady has deceased here,' he considered her for a moment before pulling out an A4 photograph, 'do you recognise this girl?"

Her breath caught in her throat threatening to choke her as she gazed, transfixed by the photograph. Kind brown eyes peered back at her from a clear, slim face framed by white-blonde hair. She attempted to swallow the lump that had formed in her chest. After a moment she shook her head slowly, forcing a smile, "No, I don't, I'm sorry"

"O.k..' He watched her with bright, blue eyes framed by long, dark lashes, 'are you o.k? Do you need to be somewhere?"

"Oh, I guess I need to be at school, sixth form, I'm eighteen soon" she turned away to hide her flushed cheeks, entirely unsure as to why she had said that.

He smiled, bemused and obviously flattered, "Well, do you need a lift?"

She allowed him a half smile, "That's o.k, I could do with the exercise anyway Officer..."

"Bennett,' He squeeze her hand lightly, 'Nice to meet you"

"You too, I'm Felicity' she breathed, feeling a little dizzy, 'I have to go. Thank you" She turned away, her long curls whipping behind her in the wind.

"Felicity?' She turned back to Officer Bennett, and tried to ignore the small flash of toned stomach as a breeze lifted his shirt, 'I'm about to turn twenty-one. Not that many years between us are there?"

Smiling shyly, she raises her hand in a small wave, before turning away and walking quickly toward the town. The wind tossed the skirt of her floral sundress about her knees so that she had to hold it down, and tears streamed from her eyes. She stopped suddenly, so that people had to veer around her, muttering and knocking her with bags or elbows.

She sat abruptly at a bench and put her face into her hands. It was her. It was definitely her. The girl that she was in her dream. Dead. She wondered how it had happened. She took a deep, shaking breath and stood with determination. She had done nothing wrong, she told herself, each step to school faster and harder. It was just a coincidence, she had been in her room, asleep the whole time, for goodness sakes!

*

Stretching her arms and yawning, Felicity sidled into the kitchen.

"Morning Mum" she glanced up at her and stopped. On the front page of her mothers newspaper, was a headline 'LOCAL GIRL MURDERED!'. Maybe it would say how, she thought desperately, attempting to read the story surreptitiously.

Her mum peered at her from around the newspaper before placing it onto the counter and folding her arms, "Can I help you, Fliss?"

"Umm...' Felicity shook her head, pasting on a smile, 'no, not at all."

Her mum headed over to the sink, planting a kiss on her head as she passed. She watched her for a moment before snatching up the newspaper, her eyes scanning the page.

Her name was - had been - Louise Mason. She was sixteen. Felicity swallowed the lump in her throat. Ah, here it is, she noted, her heart pounding in her chest.

Shot. She suddenly couldn't breathe for a moment. Louise had been shot. With her hands and feet bound with rope. Felicity felt sick. It was the same, the description sounded exactly the same as the barn that she had dreamed of.

She dropped the newspaper onto the counter top as though it had scolded her. She couldn't bear to look at it any longer; all that she could see was the flash of a gun, and the terror in Louise Mason's eyes.

*

Enjoy an extract of the upcoming third book in The Felicity Lawrence Series:

Winters Kill

Winters Kill

Prologue

Some people kill for passion. Some for revenge. But most people. Most people who kill, do it for the fame. The recognition.

It was snowing, the ground crunching beneath the heavy walking boots with each trudging step. The bag dragged behind them, leaving a trail of thick, pink liquid, which had started out red; the steadily falling flakes would soon cover that up.

They emerged from the cover of the trees, looking stealthily around them, and upon seeing that not a soul was around, they continued swiftly to the centre of the field.

Breathing heavily by the time they got there, they opened the bag, grinning manically as they left their mark.

*

Chapter One

Felicity pulled her hair up into a top knot and breathed a sigh heavy with the pressures of studying.

She had been at university for six months now, and whilst she loved it, between lectures, classes and visiting her mum in hospital, she barely had time to actually revise, let alone do the things that most normal eighteen-year olds did in their first year of university.

Her bedroom door flew open, revealing her flat mate, Louisa, with wet hair hanging to her waist and a small towel wrapped around her, revealing her long, toffee coloured limbs.

"Are you coming out tonight?" She demanded, arching a perfectly plucked brow at her.

"You know I can't Lou" Felicity sighed, her heart sinking even as she said it.

"Come on!' she moved to sit beside her, wrapping an arm over her shoulders, 'you know you want to! You're wasting the best years of your life right now."

"This is the only time I get to study"

Louisa growled, grabbing Felicity by the shoulders and turning her to face her, "Listen, everybody knows that the first year is the settling in period. Nobody expects a perfect record. What they do expect, however, is a perfect party attendance!"

She grinned. Felicity felt her resolve weaken. Louisa was right. Felicity worked really hard, and she was probably the only one who did. After the last year, she deserved to have a good time.

"Fine' she announced, standing decisively, 'but you need to help me get ready because I have no idea what people wear at these things!"

Louisa clapped with delight, throwing open Felicity's wardrobe with a flourish.

*

Felicity frowned, pulling at the skirt, which was more of a belt and had come from Louisa's wardrobe, and shook one of her three inch heels to dislodge the snow that was steadily building.

It was an unseasonably cold March, with snowfalls all over the country, and right not, she was regretting her decision to leave the halls, rather than stay in her room with films on her laptop and a mug of hot chocolate.

They reached the student union bar and Louisa turned, clutching at Felicity's hand with a reassuring smile, before pushing through the double doors.

A wall of sound hit them, knocking the breath out of Felicity. The music, something from the early noughties, was loud, sending an earthquake through the false-wood floor. A crowd of people was buzzing like a swarm of bees, and she soon realised that they were queueing at the bar.

Her feet moved quickly, as she was dragged into a run by Louisa, who seemed to be heading for a table of three boys and two girls who raised their drinks jovially.

"Fliss' Louisa shouted into her ear, pointing at people as she spoke, 'this is George, Maisy, Ethan, Andy and Helen. They all live in our building, just not in our halls."

She leant towards them, obviously introducing Felicity, and they all waved, shouting silent greetings. Felicity smiled back, squeezing onto the one seat that had been presented to the two of them.

Shandy pints were pushed towards them enthusiastically, drops spilling over the edges of the glance, and, in the ruddy smiling faces of those around her, Felicity began to feel… right.

*

Felicity staggered out of the bar, into the frozen night air, and ended up at a wooden bench somehow. She noticed, moments after she sat, that her leg was close to a bird poo, and for some reason she was simultaneously disgusted and amused.

"Are you ok?"

Felicity glanced up as Helen sat neatly on the bench beside her. She had had at least as many drinks as Felicity, but for some reason she seemed completely sober.

"This is my first party" Felicity answered, although it didn't sound like that.

Helen laughed; "How are you finding it?"

Felicity nodded her response; if she opened her mouth she wasn't sure that only words would come out.

Helen stared at her, her blonde hair a halo around her dainty face, and her blue eyes bright, "I recognise you."

Felicity frowned, "Maybe you've seen me when you came to visit Lou."

Helen shook her head, "No, you're the girl. The psychic one' she grinned, though it didn't seem to kind now, 'the one who summons death"

Felicity couldn't move, and she didn't know whether it was the snow, or the fear that was freezing her from the centre outwards.

She stood abruptly, nausea pooling in her stomach like acid, and began to walk on numb feet in the general direction of the halls.

She could hear Helen calling her name, confusion clouding her voice, or was it mocking, and she turned to look at her, backing into a field that she couldn't remember being anywhere near to where she lived.

Helen screamed, her face almost clownish in the half light of the moon. Felicity's hands moved instinctively to her face, feeling around, until she realised that she was staring over her shoulder, mouth still open as if she was yelling silently.

Slowly, on shaking legs, though she didn't know why, Felicity turned.

Her stomach clenched, and she pressed a hand to her lips.

The face stared at her, eyes wide open. The crisp, white snow was streaked with pink and dark brown blood.

Snow Angel.

The Author

Claire Taylor currently lives in Essex with her husband, two sons and mother and father-in-law – not to mention four chickens and two dogs! She dreams of living in Devon one day, and turning writing into a full time career – but for now she enjoys looking after those in need at a Care Home.

Get In Touch

Email: towriteistodream@outlook.com

Website: clairetaylorwriting.godaddysites.com

Twitter: @ClaireTauthor1

Instagram: c.i.bear

Facebook: Claire Taylor Fiction @claireitaylor